High Times and Low Lifes at the Sand Bar Town Saloons

By

Scott L. Weeden

Order this book online at www.trafford.com
or email orders@trafford.com

Most Trafford titles are also available at major online book retailers.

Acknowledgements:

For quotes at the beginning of each chapter:
Th e Purcell Register, Purcell, McClain County, Oklahoma

For the newspaper archives:
Oklahoma Historical Society, Archives and Manuscript Division

For the cover photograph:
Western History Collections, University of Oklahoma

Print information available on the last page.

ISBN: 978-1-4251-4340-4 (sc)
ISBN: 978-1-4251-6461-4 (hc)

Trafford rev. 01/06/2022

 www.trafford.com

North America & international
toll-free: 844-688-6899 (USA & Canada)
fax: 812 355 4082

Dedication

Dedicated to the memory of my great grandfather, David W. Weeden, and great uncle, Layfaette "Lafe" Weeden who were two pioneers in Indian Territory and early Oklahoma. Dave, born in 1847, and Lafe, born in 1845, both in Ohio, exemplify the rough-hewn, hardy souls that settled the Old West. This is also dedicated to my grandfather, Lewis Ernest Weeden, who was driving a freight wagon pulled by oxen in Indian Territory in 1886 when he was 12 years old, and to my cousin, Austin Walter Weedn, without whom much of the Weeden/Weedn family history would most likely still be undiscovered.

Acknowledgements

I acknowledge my mother, Marion Louise Zwicker Weeden, who has been and continues to be a constant source of encouragement in my writing career; Al Arlian, who supported me in sending out my manuscript; Kristina Langston and Alan Goldsberry, who have always provided encouragement; and Laurel Natale, Anne Townsend, Sandy Weider and Kay Folk, my critique group in Houston who made such a difference in my writing. I also acknowledge my sister, Lynne Kay Holkan, my brothers, Jon Mark and Ronald Lewis "Lew" Weeden, and their families; the extended members of the Weeden/Weedn family; all of my myriad friends from Landmark Education and the Holiday Project; my high school English teacher, Mabel "Peaches" Lewis; everyone who said, "I can't wait to read your book;" and Allison Taylor, whose magic put the finishing touch on the book.

Saloon History

The Sand Bar Saloon did actually exist in the Chickasaw Nation in the late 19th Century, where it was built on a sandbar in the South Canadian River. Winding between the Chickasaw Nation and the Unassigned Lands at that time, the river became the dividing line between Purcell, Indian Territory, and Lexington, Oklahoma Territory. The basic information about the Sand Bar Saloon is included in the book woven into the fictitious story.

The characters based loosely on Dave and Lafe Weeden as well as their saloons are fictitious. However, several of the situations described in the book are based on old family stories.

Preface

D.W. Sweden thought he had found the perfect way to make he and his brother, Lincoln, a good deal of money by building and running a saloon in the middle of the river that ran between Purcell and Lexington.

Seeking other partners, D.W. had discussed the matter at some length. Building it right on the sandbar in the middle of the South Canadian River, they would bring in the business from both towns and make a killing selling their home-distilled whiskey.

They had a few obstacles to overcome such as rains and flooding, and getting the customers to the saloon - and home again. They would be the first to do so. Others would follow when they saw the profit the Sweden boys were bringing in.

"Tell us not that the Indians are not becoming civilized. We saw a Cheyenne chief buying a tablecloth yesterday of the finest fabric."
-- Republican Traveler.
"Probably so. To sell tablecloths to the Indians is an every day occurrence here, but after noticing the way most of them wear them, one can hardly call that method civilized." -- Purcell Register.
"The Register surely hasn't the gall to insinuate that poor Lo would wear a tablecloth for a breech-clout." -- Hesperian.
"No, but many of them seem to think that a tablecloth makes a good shawl or blanket."
. . . The Purcell Register, Feb. 4, 1888

Chapter 1

Springtime in the Chickasaw Nation is always a sight to behold. All those trees starting to sprout leaves, the grass turning green, the storms blowing through. But this spring was different. Instead of the sweet music of the blue jays and mockingbirds echoing across the valley, the sounds of hammers driving spikes and men cursing the Santa Fe Railroad drifted through the cottonwood trees along the South Canadian River.

The Canadian River Valley is famous for having one of the most treacherous rivers in the country. As the river winds between Oklahoma and Indian territories, you may suddenly find yourself in the most quicksand ridden stretch of riverbottom this side of nowhere. If you aren't real careful, nowhere is where you'll end up.

In 1887, the railroad was just pushing through the territory and the last link between Kansas and Texas was being completed there in the riverbottom. Me and my brother, Lincoln Sweden, had wandered into Indian Territory a couple of years before, trying to get away from the press of civilization, or something like that. Lincoln had settled over in Pottawatomie country while I was in the Chickasaw Nation a few miles west of Purcell. Our favorite spot to meet and pass the time of day was

1

on Red Hill, a bright spot of red clay on the northern edge of Purcell. I always enjoyed the view from there because nobody could sneak up on us either.

Off to the north, we could see the railroaders working to cross the river. It seemed like every time they tried to sink a log for their bridge, the log just kept going out of sight. Those folks spent a lot of time figuring out that some of that quicksand just didn't have no bottom. Well, all this feverish activity had got me to thinking.

"Hey, Linc, you still have that special deck of cards?" I asked him. I was laying on my back on the green grass, watching those fluffy clouds moving slowly across a deep blue sky.

He raised his left eyebrow. "As I recall, those cards got us run out of Kansas City. What's the special occasion?"

I ignored his obvious lack of enthusiasm for my newest project. "You still got that old Indian blanket?"

His right eyebrow rose. "Yeah."

"Don't you just love the view from Red Hill? This is wide open country. Why, there's fruit ripe for the pluckin' everywhere."

"Look here, D.W., I don't like it when you start changing the subject. I swear I'm going to disown you one of these days."

"Now, Linc. Have we ever got caught?"

"No, but we've lived in four different states over the past fifteen years and we're not welcome in very many of those. That's beside the point. There isn't any fruit to pluck around here in the springtime. Have you been eating those Osage oranges again? That's about the only fruit you'll find around here."

Linc was pacing up and down on the south side of the crest of the hill on a flat section of rock. I could see the double ribbons of the railroad tracks stretching off to Texas. The roadbed work was just beginning on the riverbank below the bluff. I could see my brother could use a little more convincing.

"Now, look at you Linc. That pair of pants you have on has seen a lot better days. If you put one more sweat stain on that beat up old Stetson, the dried dirt and sweat will be the only thing holding it together. And, that plaid shirt of yours almost looks like a solid, dingy gray. A golden opportunity is bein' laid in our laps. Besides, how bright can these fellas be? Look at 'em. They cut more logs than Abe Lincoln ever thought about."

"Why can't we open a store like that Wantland fellow down there?" Linc replied, pointing to a tent a few miles to the south. "Hell, he's already got plans to build a wooden store right down at the foot of this hill. He'll have all the business in this end of the Chickasaw Nation by the time he's done. He's going to put Purcell on the map. And, we can't even buy a pair of boots from him."

"Linc. That's exactly what I'm talkin' about. Look, these railroad guys don't know us from Adam. They definitely don't have any place to spend their money and most of the gamblers haven't come this far up the line yet. We can go down there and relieve them of their boredom and money. Not necessarily in that order, of course. By the time they catch on, the railroad will be finished and they'll be on their way somewhere else."

He slowly turned to me, his eyes narrowed. "All right. But, what do you want the blanket for?"

"You remember our Runnin' Bear dodge? I'll get 'em started this evenin' and you show up in a couple of days. Payday is Friday. I'll set up a faro game and let them win a little. I'll let them know about Runnin' Bear. They'll be primed by the time Runnin' Bear shows up. You want some wampum. I want some wampum. These guys have got wampum. Of course, I'll need a couple of bottles of fire water to go along with that. You just make sure you look like a damn Indian by the time you get back here."

Linc shook his head. "As long as we've been in Indian Territory, you've been trying to get money and land out of the government by pretending to be a Choctaw. You weren't born in Mississippi. You were born in Ohio. You haven't collected one red cent. Maybe if you quit laying around getting drunk with the Indians, you could make something of yourself."

"And you're gonna do that, I suppose?"

"You're damn right," Linc said, scratching his growth of beard. "I been doing a little horse doctoring over with the Pottawatomies. Now, a few folks are starting to come to me to fix them up, too. I could become a good doctor."

"You ain't no doctor. Why, you cain't even tell the front end of a horse from the back end."

Linc stopped and looked at me. "Is that so?" Without another word, he put his foot in the stirrup of his saddle and swung his leg over the horse's back.

"Now, don't get your hackles up. Hell, I was just pullin' your leg. If you really want to get started doctorin', then this could be your grubstake."

"I don't know, D.W. One of these days we've got to find a better way to make money."

"Just you be back here in a couple of days and we'll take care of business," I told him as he rode away. "And we're gonna skin us some beavers," I added under my breath.

I got out my spyglasses and squatted down on my haunches. The depot station at the foot of the hill looked almost complete and a lot of the railroad hands were sitting around down on the platform. There were still a couple of hours of daylight left, so I laid down and waited for the sun to set.

The cool of the evening woke me up. I shivered a little as I rolled up into a sitting position. Here I was, just turned 40. I was getting way too old to be working for a living but I didn't have much choice. What I needed was a scheme that would feather my nest for years to come. Of course, like Linc said, I'd been looking for one of those schemes four states ago. Still and all, I could never pass up a chance to build my fortunes.

I grabbed the horse's reins and started walking down the back side of the hill towards Purcell proper. A bright red sunset lit up the white, puffy clouds, turning them a dozen different shades of pink. By the time I reached the road that ran down the lots that had been laid out for the town of Purcell, the sun was well below the horizon. The track down the bluff to the riverbed was already dark, but a few fires were flickering around the depot. A light mist was rising off the river and the frogs and crickets were busy serenading the crew. A coyote was howling off to the west.

The fire furthest from the depot seemed to have the rowdiest bunch, so I headed over there.

"Hello, the fire," I called out.

"What the hell do you want?"

I smiled. I knew I was in the right place. "I was lookin' for a little palaver. Don't get too many white men out this way."

"If that's all you want, go find a quiltin' bee somewheres," one of the men called back, setting off a round of guffaws.

"I like to do my talkin' over a deck of cards," I said, tossing a box of worn cards in their midst.

One of the railroaders stood up and looked me over. He was a short man with a full beard and a scar that ran across his right cheek. He snorted, "If you don't mind some low stakes, I guess you can join us."

I tied my horse to a cottonwood and pulled a blanket off the back of my saddle. Spreading it out on the ground near the fire, I pulled out my faro cloth and my gambling change. I could see three or four of them with their heads together, planning my demise.

Faro was one of those games that was easy to lose if you knew what cards were coming up. As the dealer, I was the banker and, as they could see, I really didn't have much bank. All thirteen spades were painted on the cloth. Each person would place a bet on one of the cards. Suits aren't important in this game, just rank. If the first card was a seven and the second card was a five, any player who bet on the seven lost and any player who bet on the five won. If someone bet on the nine, then I'd have to turn over two more cards to find out if they won or lost. If two fives came up on the same turn, then a split occurs and the dealer

6

keeps half the bets. A player could copper his bet, which meant he was betting to lose with the first card.

After a couple of runs through the deck, I knew these guys would be easy pickings. I really had to struggle to find creative ways to lose. That's how bad they were. Anyway, I started setting them up for my return trip on payday.

"These cards just ain't runnin' my way tonight. I ain't never seen the luck go agin me so bad."

"Maybe that's why you're livin' in this Godforsaken hellhole," one of them sneered at me. "Your luck done run out."

"Nah. That ain't it. I know what my problem is. I ain't got my lucky blanket."

That started a new round of laughter. "The way you play, the only thing you'll need a blanket for is to wrap yourself in when they bury you."

"No. Really. All I need is my lucky blanket."

"What makes you think this damn blanket is so lucky?" another one of them asked, winking to his buddies.

"Why it's a medicine blanket. It's got good Injun medicine. I stole it from ol' chief Runnin' Bear. A fat ol' Comanche. Why that blanket has survived fires and floods and cyclones and damn near everythin' else. It's the luckiest piece of material I have ever seen."

"If it was so lucky, how did you get it away from Runnin' Bear? And where the hell is he?" one of them thought to ask. "How come you still got this blanket?"

"I told you it was lucky. If it hadn't been for that blanket, I would have never stayed ahead of that ol' chief for nigh onto three years. He swore revenge on me and has been a-chasin' me ever since. Don't worry, though, I ain't seen him for a couple of months now, so I imagine he's finally give up on the chase."

"That don't sound too lucky to me," scar-face said.

"Yeah, but I ain't never lost a card game on that blanket," I told him.

The whole damn group started laughing at me as I paid out

my last twenty cents to someone after I slipped the soda card back in the deck so he could win. "Well, I'm tapped out."

"Come back anytime," they laughed. "It was great havin' a palaver with you."

"I'll be back Friday night," I said, rolling up my cloth. "I'll get me a stake and I'll bring my lucky blanket and then I'll show you."

I grabbed my deck of cards and my other blanket and shuffled out of there with my head hung down, muttering to myself. I rode a little ways away from the fire and surveyed what they were doing. I could see they were laughing and having a wonderful time talking about the crazy man and his Injun blanket. Ah, why couldn't there be more railroaders in the territory, I thought to myself as I rode home.

By the time Friday rolled around, I was as ready as I could get. I was sitting on my back porch when Linc rode up. He was decked out in a buckskin shirt with deerhide pants, moccasins and an old cavalry hat with an eagle feather in it. I could see that he remembered to shave so he'd look a little bit like an Indian. He didn't look at all excited.

"I must be crazy doing this again," he told me.

"You say that every time we do somethin' excitin' and you always enjoy it afterwards. You got the blanket I see. The cards? How about the whiskey?" I smiled as he held up our special deck and two jugs. "You been practicin' with your bow and arrows."

"You know I'm no damned good with a bow," he complained.

"You'll do just fine. These guys wouldn't know how to play faro if the cards were turned face up. We could probably take all their money without the dodge."

"Then why in tarnation are we doing this? I can just go home now."

"I need to make sure no one comes lookin' for us later. We still got to live here peaceable with the Indians for a few more

8

years."

"All right. Let's get this over with. When do you want to start?"

"Oh, I figure a couple of hours after sundown will be fine. It'll give 'em a chance to get likkered up and I can get the low rollers out of the game and the big money on the blanket. You shoot a couple of arrows around the fire, give off a few war whoops and that should scatter 'em long enough for you to ride in and claim your blanket. Try to put the first arrow in the fire."

"What if I miss?"

"Then, don't hit me," I said, getting a little peeved at his bad attitude.

"I'm not pulling any lead out of your butt if this goes wrong this time," he said, looking me straight in the eye.

"Have I ever led you wrong?"

"Damn right you have," he said, getting a little riled up.

"I promise you there'll be no problems this time."

He shook his head and sat down on the porch. We practiced the rest of the afternoon with the cards until I had the finer points of the design in my mind again.

We rode the few miles to Purcell in silence. About a mile away from town, Linc pulled up. "Well, white man, this is where we part company."

"I'll take good care of your blanket, Runnin' Bear. When I stand up and take my hat off, you'll know the blanket is primed and ready to go."

"Hmmmmmm," was his only reply.

By the time I reached the riverbed, a good-sized group had gathered near a big cottonwood. The fire was burning good and the whole gang was just waiting for their prize pelt to arrive. I wasn't about to disappoint them. Only two or three of them had guns on and I hoped that the guns were more for show than anything else. Someone had brought out some dice and two or three of them were hunched over watching the roll of the bones. As soon as they saw me coming, though, the attention turned to me.

"Here he comes now, big chief dirt grubber."

"Is that Runnin' Bear I see coming up behind you, Runnin' Dog."

"Hey, I brought my lucky blanket, too."

I shrugged off all their words and made like it didn't bother me at all. I took out that worn old blanket and spread it on the ground. It was a pretty good blanket. It was black with a white buffalo in the middle and various other symbols that must have meant something to someone somewhere. The only thing it represented to me was a fleecing. That old blanket hadn't seen a good washing in years, which just added to all the fun they were poking at me.

The faro game started out a little slow. Once the jugs got passed around, the action picked up considerably. By the time the jugs were empty, everyone there was in a fine mood. I ran four or five of them out of the game real quick. Simple suggestions got them to play to losing hands. I made sure that the banker wasn't taking in too much money.

"See. I told you guys this was my lucky blanket," I said after the first hour of playing. "I'm doing a whole lot better tonight than I did the other evenin'."

"That won't last too long," scar-face said. I could tell he wasn't happy with the way the cards had been running.

More of them dropped by the wayside and my winnings were starting to add up. The grumbles at the edge of the crowd were beginning. I could tell the better players had been holding back, watching me play. Now, they started moving into the game. It was a lot tougher winning against these guys and they started eating into my funds. As my winnings started edging down, the pots kept edging upwards. I could tell that most of the money was on the blanket now and I didn't think I could beat these guys.

"I need to change positions," I said, standing up and taking my hat off to wipe the sweat out of my eyes.

An arrow came whistling out of the dark, scattering embers from the fire.

"What the hell is that?" one of the drunks mumbled.

"It looks like a damn arrow," another said.

"It is a damn arrow," the third one added.

A second arrow struck the ground between one drunk's outstretched legs. He couldn't have gotten his eyes any wider if he had tried.

I grabbed it up. "Oh, my God. It's Comanche. Runnin' Bear is here and he's on the warpath. Anyone who's touched his sacred blanket is a dead man. Let's get the hell out of here. He takes scalps."

The first circle of railroaders nearest the fire, turned and ran into the darkness as word of the attack spread throughout the camp. Drunks were fighting each other to get away from the firelight. One drunk tripped face first over a log as the third arrow came swooping into the melee. The poor, unlucky soul was just getting up off the ground when the arrow hit him in the fleshiest part of his butt. He jumped straight up, which was the wrong move to make with an arrow in the posterior. I swear you could have heard that scream all the way to Kansas. That's all it took for the whole crowd to break and run. Elbows and assholes were flailing away in every direction. I hightailed it for the river.

The guy with the arrow in his butt was kneeling with his butt in the air. He was crying and choking at the same time, "Don't scalp me. I ain't got that much hair left. I wasn't on no blanket."

I almost felt sorry for him as I left the circle of light. About that time Linc came riding in with his tomahawk waving in the air and warwhoops adding to the railroaders' fears. He cut a fine figure in the firelight as he reared the horse back a couple to times. I would have stayed and admired him, but I was in a hurry to cross the Canadian. He jumped out of the saddle and reached down and picked up the whole bundle -- blanket, cards, faro cloth and money. He then headed for the river after me.

"White man thief. Scalp look good on teepee."

In less than thirty seconds, the whole dodge was complete. Not a shot had been fired, much to our relief. This was by far one of the best scams we had ever run. Once we cleared the fire-light, I swung up behind Linc and we rode for the middle of the river. We approached a stretch of riverbottom that we knew had quicksand. We climbed down from the horse, laughing so hard we could barely stand.

After emptying the contents of the blanket into a sack, I walked to the edge of the quicksand with my weight on my toes, like I'd been running. I took the blanket and sailed it out over the quicksand. It slowly settled on the sand until it was floating on top. Then, I took my hat and tossed it out in front of the blanket. I pulled a pair of moccasins out of my shirt and slipped out of my boots. After I put on the moccasins, I backed out of there along the same line as my boot tracks to make it look like Running Bear had chased the gambler to their deaths. When I was close enough to the horse, Linc jumped down with his moc-casins on so that those prints would be a lot deeper to indicate the Indian had dismounted to pursue his foe. We then pulled the horse up along side, remounted and left the vicinity.

Those railroaders were sure to come looking for their money in the morning and the only thing they would find left of the Indian and the white man would be a stretch of quicksand with a couple of funeral markers on it.

Sure enough, the next day, the howls of the railroad men could be heard for miles. You would've thought every Comanche in the territory had been there the night before. Old scar-face was carrying a rope with a noose at the end, swearing revenge and pointing to the cottonwood where he was going to string me up.

They needed a doctor for the man with the arrow in his butt, so Linc was called to minister to the poor fellow. It was hard for him to keep a straight face while he listened to the track crew. They didn't have the slightest idea of what really happened.

Linc was very careful as he cut the arrowhead out of the guy. That was Linc's first job as a surgeon. I knew this dodge would help his medical business. I guess doctoring all those cows and pigs must have done him some good. Anyway, he offered the arrowhead to the guy so he could pass it onto his children and grandchildren about how he had survived an Indian attack.

Over the course of the operation, Linc kept telling them that he didn't hold out much likelihood of them finding anybody out on that riverbed. Only a damn fool would venture out in the Canadian after dark. And, as for Indians, well they all looked alike and he had trouble telling them apart.

About that time, the search party came back from the river draggin' the blanket. They were cussing up a storm. They told everybody where they found it. The hat was further out in the quicksand and nobody was foolhardy enough to get it so they left it there. Everybody agreed that the Indian and that fool gambler had gotten their just rewards. Too bad they had taken the railroaders' rewards with them as well.

On top of that, Linc got five dollars for his doctoring. Maybe there's hope for him yet. We each got a little over two hundred dollars from the blanket. And, Running Bear? Well, nobody's heard from him since.

"The Way of the Transgressor
"The risks that men will run to get the almighty dollar seems to
be unlimited and perpetual. One would think that the number of
men arrested in this Territory for peddling whiskey would cause a
complete halt in its traffic.
"But it seems to make no difference. No sooner are one lot well
on their way towards Ft. Smith, than a new brigade of candidates
for the penitentiary spring up and flourish for a while, only to be cut
down in the height of their glory by the officers of the law.
"Verily though 'the way of the transgressor be hard' the road is
well traveled."

. . . The Purcell Register, Nov. 23, 1887

Chapter 2

The sounds of civilization in the territory mixed with those
of Mother Nature always seemed to bring me pure pleasure - the
shrill whistle of a train echoing down the Canadian River bottom; the rustle of the leaves on the cottonwood trees at the foot
of Red Hill; the shuffling of cards; and, the gurgle of whiskey
being poured into glasses.

That last wonderful sound always brought the refrains of
that old song back to me: "Rye whiskey, rye whiskey, rye
whiskey, I cry. If I don't get rye whiskey, I surely will die."

Purcell was now a hotbed of activity. With the railroad and
one of the few fords across the river, the town attracted all types
of businesses and businessmen. Then, late in 1888, business
really began to boom when rumors of a land run brought spec-
ulators into the territory from all over the country. It was the
finest time I ever had making corn liquor. I didn't even have to
sell it to the saloons. I was selling it off the back of my wagon.
I couldn't keep up with the demand. Over those few months, I
must have burned the blackjack oaks off two acres of woodland
to keep my still going.

It helped that I had some friends who could keep me posted
on when the marshal and the local sheriff were out of town. As

13

long as my main competitors were being hauled off to Ft. Smith, then I was doing fine.

Every man that walked the streets of the "Queen City of the Chickasaw Nation" carried a pistol, a rifle or a knife or all three. It's plumb amazing more people weren't killed with all the liquored up cowboys, Indians and townfolks parading up and down Main Street. No man's outfit was complete without something like a Colt Peacemaker .45 strapped to his hip and a Winchester .44-.40 rifle cradled in his arms or hanging from his saddle.

I was partial to an old Colt Navy .36. When it came to protecting my whiskey runs, that sawed-off 12-gauge shotgun was a lot more effective than a rifle.

As more and more people heard about the land run, Purcell just kept getting more crowded. Winter never was an especially good time to move into the territory and 1888-89 was no different. Most of the folks there were chasing some dream of free land and a new start. Two or three families were living in dugouts in the bluffs of the Canadian River. There was even one Negro family starving to death along Walnut Creek. Such a sad state of affairs was everywhere to be seen in the territory.

That was the winter I almost got a one-way ticket out of the territory. One of the biggest whiskey peddlers in Indian Territory wore a skirt. Belle Starr was one mean-spirited woman. She ran with the best of the badmen for years. She hobnobbed with Cole Younger and the James Gang. By the time I had the misfortune to make her acquaintance, she was 40 years old and looked like she'd been around the territory an awful long time.

She came sashaying up Main Street in Purcell one Friday evening. I was sitting on the tailgate of my wagon in an alleyway across from Brisco's livery. A couple of young bucks with hoglegs tied down were trailing along behind her. Her hips were fairly wide and her corset was fairly tight. She wasn't but about five-foot, three or four-inches tall and she didn't flinch at anything. Her dark hair was pinned back under her riding hat.

From a distance, she cut a fine figure of a woman. Being the man that I was, I watched her coming down the street. She walked right up to me and put her hands on her hips like she was ready to do some business. I hopped off the wagon smartly, nodded my head and looked back into those pale eyes. She turned to the side and glanced back over her shoulder at the two bucks. I could see she had a six-shooter strapped to her right hip. That was a signal that she wasn't your typical shop owner's wife. At least one of us was up to no good and for a change, it wasn't me.

"You, D.W. Sweden?" she asked, her mouth a grim line in an otherwise bland face.

"That I am."

"You got some whiskey to sell?"

"That depends. I don't usually sell whiskey to ladies on the street."

She turned her head and spat into the dusty street. "I was told you make the best moonshine in these here parts."

I looked up and down the street trying to figure out what in the hell was going on. "Now who would have told you something like that, ma'am?"

"None of your damned business. Let's just say that some people around here keep track of these things for me."

I narrowed my eyes and looked from her to her two companions and back again. "To whom am I addressin' myself?"

She pursed her lips. I could tell she was sizing me up. "My name's Belle Starr."

My eyebrows shot up when I heard that and I started looking for the nearest hole to crawl into. Now, I'm about six-feet tall and pretty good sized. But the sound of her name got me to feeling about half that size. I wasn't looking for no trouble from the Bandit Queen. I cleared my throat. "It just so happens that I've already sold my last jug. I don't really have no more with me."

"Take me into one of these saloons that has your moonshine and buy me a drink of your liquor," she said. "I'm tired of you wasting my time."

I could tell immediately that I wasn't about to sweet talk my way out of this one and she was in no mind to take any other answer except, "Yes, ma'am."

One of the young bucks moved his coat back away from his gun and the other one motioned me to lead the way. My shotgun was under the front seat of the wagon and I knew my gunfighting skills had flown away with whatever small amount of courage I might have had. We strolled into the Golden Stag Saloon. Not too many folks in there, but everyone of them swiveled their heads around to watch our little procession. A couple of them must have recognized Belle because they leaned over to the others at their table and whispered something to them.

"Look, D.W., I've done bought all the whiskey from you I can. What the hell do you want now?" Hosea Thibodeaux shot back at me while he polished a glass.

"Well," I gulped, "It ain't fer me. The little lady wants a sip of my best blend."

Hosea laughed, "Hell, you ain't got a best blend."

Belle took her gun out of her holster and put it on the bar. Then, she gave me and Hosea a look that would have cooked a goose without a stove. "I ain't no 'little' lady and I won't take no more of your wiseass remarks. Bartender, if you want to live to see your children grow up, then you'll damn well shut up and pour that drink."

Hosea looked at the gun, Belle and me. "What in the hell is going on here?"

She glared at him. "Are you deaf? Shut up and pour before me and my boys take you and this whole place apart board by board."

One by one, the remaining bar patrons had been seeking a hasty exit to the rear of the saloon. By the time Hosea got a jug up to the shot glass, the place was empty except for Belle, her boys, the bartender and the bootlegger. Hosea's hand was shaking so bad he put more whiskey on the bar than he did in the glass. He didn't waste any time cleaning up the mess. He wandered aimlessly towards the far end of the bar. The last I saw of him was the southern end of his northbound carcass. I must admit, though, I was quite envious of him at that moment.

Even though there wasn't a breeze in the place, my coattails were flapping around like a crow in a cyclone. Must have been that I couldn't stop my knees from knocking.

Belle picked up the glass and swirled the liquor around. With a quick flick of her wrist, she emptied the glass and gulped the whiskey down. The left corner of her mouth turned up. "That's damn good drinking. Sit down and let's talk business."

She walked over to a table and sat down. Pointing to a chair, she kicked it away from the table and motioned me to sit. The two young bucks leaned against the wall behind her. I didn't say anything. It would have taken the second coming of Christ to get a word out of me and she was a far sight removed from Him. I wobbled over to the chair and fell into it.

"The reason I came here today was to offer you a deal," she said. "My boys peddle their whiskey all over Indian Territory so I hear about anybody that sells rotgut anywhere around. I'd heard you made some mighty fine brew and was pretty good at avoiding the marshals. So, I come over to find out for myself. I must admit, your stuff does have a kick and it's got a little different taste. Now, here's the deal. Either work for me or find yourself another way to make a living. If you keep on making moonshine on your own, you might not live long enough to have another drink."

"I'll be glad to sell you as much as you'd like . . ."

Ka-bloom.

The windows rattled and my ears couldn't stop ringing from the sound of the gunshot. From under the table where I had accidentally fallen in my haste to get out of the line of fire, I peered up through the gunsmoke at a very unhappy woman. I looked across the room at where a bullet hole had suddenly appeared in the spittoon at the end of the bar.

"You have a very bad way of irritating me," she said, her eyes narrowed and her gun steady as a rock. "Get up off that damned floor."

I pushed myself back into the chair with nary a word. My knees weren't shaking anymore because every muscle in my body had tensed up and locked in place. I couldn't take my eyes off the end of that damned gun and she knew it.

"Now, I take care of my people and I keep 'em out of Judge Parker's court as much as possible," Belle said, as though this was the everyday way of doing business. "I've got a bunch of contacts in the Chickasaw and Seminole nations that could use a good whiskey supply. I pay good money and the more moonshine you make, the more money you get. Any whiskey you sell hereabouts is mine. I get the money and you get a cut. You savvy?"

I nodded my head rapidly up and down.

"I see you finally got my message. Now, what's it going to be?"

I had trouble clearing my throat. "That doesn't sound like I've got much choice," I finally got out.

She threw her head back and laughed out loud. "I'm glad to see you like my way of doing business."

"Great. How will I know you won't sell me down the river?"

"Just try to do business with someone else and the only thing that will be going down the river is pieces of your body. That's a promise."

"What a deal."

"I knew you'd see it my way," she said, laughing as she slid her gun into her holster. She headed for the door with her two guards in tow. They looked back at me, grinning like cats with canaries in their mouths.

Lucky for me, my business and my health, that was the last time I ever saw Belle Starr. She met her untimely demise from the business end of a shotgun. On Feb. 3, 1889, somebody shot her from ambush. No, it wasn't my shotgun. It didn't take me long at all to fire up the still for a batch of whiskey to toast her memory.

"1888 ought to be a good year for poker players. It contains three of a kind."

. . . The Purcell Register, Feb. 4, 1888

Chapter 3

The last day of spring 1889 was dawning and the weather in the territory was up to its old tricks. Long before I came here, I heard that they only had three seasons in this part of the country -- winter, summer and tornado. After a few of those fast moving thunderstorms, I got a fine appreciation of the soft Indian Territory soil that allowed me to easily dig a storm cellar or two.

By then, everybody in the United States and most of the rest of the world knew that the Unassigned Lands across the river were going to be opened by land run. Purcell now had a temporary population of seven or eight thousand people. Every one of them was just waiting for the opportunity to sneak across the river and stake out a quarter section of land.

And, while they were waiting, the brethren of the green cloth were pouring into Purcell. Every train that rolled through dropped off a few more gamblers. They roamed all over town looking for the chance to relieve some poor land grubber of his life savings. Most of them didn't even bother with the saloons or gaming tents. They just set up some boards on a couple of sawhorses in an alley and started dealing misery.

Most of the time, I sat in my favorite spot on Red Hill watching the southbound Atchison, Topeka and Santa Fe bring the gamblers in from Kansas City and Wichita while the northbound Gulf, Colorado and Santa Fe brought them in from Texas and Louisiana. The trains used the roundhouse in Purcell to turn around and head back to pick up more gamblers and folks wanting to stake a new homestead.

Purcell was living high on the hog. From the top of Depot Hill down Main Street to the west, new businesses, hotels and saloons lined the dirt roadway. Wagons loaded with cotton, flour and produce rumbled through town stirring up either dust or mud, depending on whether or not a storm had blown through.

Late winter and early spring 1889 were fine times to be in the libation business in Purcell. With four saloons open to all hours, it made my business even better. Until spring planting time and early roundup, the farmers, cowboys and Indians didn't have anything else to do but have a few drinks to help while away the time.

Of course, my still was helping them with their thirst. I had that still set up in the middle of some blackjack oaks north of town along the river. It was a long ways from where I lived so that the marshals would have a harder time catching me there. Those damned trees grew thicker than prairie grass and were a thousand times tougher to move through. I had a mule, though, that could haul jugs amongst those trees without spilling nary a drop. That was why the mule's moniker was Liquid Gold. Those U.S. marshals spent most of their time looking for that dastardly whiskey runner, L.G. Swilling, without realizing he was standing outside hitched to the railing in the middle of town.

The most dangerous part of this operation was staying alive long enough to enjoy the fruits of my labors. With all those horse thieves and two-bit gunslingers wandering the streets, a decent fellow trying to earn a living could get hurt and even dead if he wasn't careful.

I spend a good part of my delivery time in the Purcell Saloon and Gaming Parlor. It was my favorite establishment since it was closest to the edge of town and had two or three handy doors for rapid exits. The saloon was in a one-story, woodframe building with roughhewn tables and chairs and a bar made out of pecan wood that had been varnished and polished till you could see your face in it. The sawdust-covered floor was splashed with brown spots where the boys that liked chewing tobacco missed the spittoons more than a few times. Through its back door ran some of the finest bank robbers and train holdup artists in the territory. Cowhands came in from all over the Indian country to sample a bit of my colored, precious, fiery liquid.

On the nights the marshals were nosing around, the games were kind of dull and all you could get to drink was a cup of coffee that would make you and your hair stand on end.

Swede Jacobsen had a nice little layout in the saloon. The front half of the building was the saloon while the gaming tables were in the back. The bar ran along the left-hand side and three long, narrow tables ran down the right side. A waist-high wall separated the saloon from the gaming parlor. An old roulette table was spaced along the back of the room. Three poker tables were set up between the dividing wall and the roulette table. A couple of other rectangular tables were set up at the end of the bar and opposite the poker tables. These were for games that needed a banker like blackjack and faro.

I somehow ended up in a poker game with an old gambler who had seen better days and four cowhands that had pretty much given up on everything except getting back at the banks and the railroads for changing the territory.

Three-Fingered Jake Hanson claimed to be a professional gambler, but the way I heard it, he was caught cheating a few too many times. After one such deal, somebody didn't take kindly to his efforts and used a Bowie knife to relieve him of the index finger on his right hand. After he was found with a couple of extra aces in his coat sleeve, a bullet was delivered through one of those aces, ruining the card and taking his middle finger with it. Old Three-Fingered Jake wasn't nearly as light fingered as he used to be, though you might say he was light a few fingers.

The four cowhands were passing through on their way to their old stomping grounds to join some friends there. Their names I would remember for a long time to come.

Tulsa Jack Blake loved his cards and wouldn't let anything

keep him from a game. He was of medium build with dark hair and a mustache. His sunburned face made him look swarthy. The man was fine as long as he was winning, but you had to step lightly when he started losing.

George "Bitter Creek" Newcomb was also called Slaughter's Kid after the rancher he worked for in the Cherokee Strip. He was short and stocky, and rather good looking with his mustache. Before damn near every hand he played, he'd recite, "I'm a wild wolf from Bitter Creek and it's my night to howl."

His best friend was a long-faced cuss named Charley Pierce. He was always scowling, which made for a great poker face. He was barrel-chested and chewed tobacco all the time. I wondered if he ever took his chaw out when he went to bed.

The other player was Black-Faced Charley Bryant. He had gotten too close to the business end of a gun when he was a teenager and the powder burns were easy to see on his left cheek. He was the meanest looking one in the bunch. He was rail-thin and his jet black eyes made a rattlesnake look downright friendly.

They had all ridden together on the Turkey Track ranch, which was south of the Cimarron River on the Sac and Fox Reservation and along the western boundary of the Creek Nation.

Tulsa Jack took the first deal. "Five card stud. No limit. Bet 'em if you got 'em."

"Look at those damn fools over there," Bitter Creek said, pointing to a group of men at the end of the bar. "They're trying to open the territory up for dirt grubbers. By the time they're done, there won't be no more free range anywhere around here."

Black-Faced Charley chimed in, "Hell, let's just go shoot 'em. That'll put an end to it."

"I'd wait a day or two before I did that," I said, drawing a glare from him. "The marshal's sittin' at the other end of the bar watchin' them."

24

Black-Faced Charley glanced around and grunted.

"Those folks call themselves Boomers," Bitter Creek said. "They're like locusts. They'll eat up the whole territory and not look back. Hell, us cowboys'll be stringing barbed wire just to keep 'em out."

Tulsa Jack bet his king while I held off raising him even though I had an ace in the hole.

"You can't stop progress, I heard," Pierce said. "Way I see it, the first thing that happens is the railroad comes through. Then towns like this one pop up all along the railroad and then the farmers come. Once they start digging postholes, the game's up."

Three-Fingered Jake had a pair of deuces showing, but bet like he was as intimidated as I was. I don't think I had ever seen any four cowboys with more shooting irons on than this quartet. Guns were hanging on their hips, across their stomachs, from their shoulders. They could have fought off the whole Cheyenne Nation by themselves.

"It's kinda like what Emmett Dalton used to tell us about his cousins, the Youngers. They rode with Jesse James and held up banks and trains all over the country. I tell you, that sounds more exciting than watching a bunch of sorry cows," Bitter Creek said.

"You wouldn't know how to hold up a tent pole with both hands," Pierce laughed. "And you'd get just about as much out of it. Tell you what, just give me the stakes you got in front of you and you'll know what it means to be held up."

"Them's fighting words," Bitter Creek said with a scowl on his face.

Three-Fingered Jake and I started to get up, but Pierce waved us back down. "He don't mean nothing by that. He's always been full of bull and braggadocio."

"Bragga what?" Tulsa Jack asked, a look of disgust on his face. "Where in hell did you come up with a word like that. Hell, I ought to shoot you myself. Use plain English."

"All it means is that he brags a lot and doesn't know what he's talking about half the time," Pierce replied. "As for shooting someone, you'd be lucky to hit the broad side of a barn."

The banter between the four of them sounded gruff, but it was obvious they knew each other pretty well. At least, I hoped they did.

"I've said it once and I'll say it again, I want to be killed in one hell-firin' minute of action. That's the way to go. Die in a blaze of glory. Might as well take out a few trains and banks along the way. At least you'd have some money to spend on your way to hell," Black-Faced Charley said, his eyes bright with the thought of his demise.

"Didn't the James and Younger gangs end up on the wrong end of the gun?" I asked, somewhat innocently.

"Yeah, but they didn't do it right," Bitter Creek said. "You got to have your hideouts set and you got to plan your jobs so that you don't get taken by surprise. What in the hell were they doing in Minnesota anyway? No place to run. No one to hide them. They were lucky they all didn't get killed."

"Emmett sure was taken with those stories. You know he's a cousin to the Youngers. His eyes always lit up when he started bragging about their deeds. I think he had them robbing more banks and trains than there were in the whole country."

I got my second ace on the last card and took the pot with a pair. I sneaked a peek at the four cowboys and they didn't seem too upset losing the first hand. I added, "I understand that Cole Younger was supposed to have had a son by Belle Starr."

"What's it to you?" Tulsa Jack shot back at me.

"I met Belle a few months ago before she was killed and she was some kind of woman," I said.

"I heard that she was a wildcat in woman's clothing," Bitter Creek said with a laugh. "That's probably what made Cole go bad."

Pierce looked at me. "What do you think about robbing banks as a profession?"

"Look. I have a hard enough time tryin' to move a little whiskey here and there in the territory. I have been incredibly lucky not to get nailed to the lamppost by the marshal. I like those low profiles. The less they see of me the better. With all these new towns, everything that's done ends up in the newspaper. Everybody's lookin' for easy money. They'd turn you in for a two-dollar reward. Until they put a bounty on moonshiners, I'll stick to that."

"I'd stand up on top of a hill somewhere and howl at them lawmen from miles away. We've ridden every ravine and hill along the Cimarron River. I bet they'd never catch us there and we could live like kings. They's a few bankers I'd like to take down a few notches," Bitter Creek said.

Pierce grabbed one of his guns. "I don't see no damn notches on your gun. What kind of a pantywaist goes after bankers?"

"Why don't you give me back that gun and I'll make damn sure you're the first notch," Bitter Creek said, grabbing at the gun. "I'll make sure they spell your name right in the newspaper."

He reached across the table and knocked about half the poker hands on the floor. They called a redeal, which was a good since my high card was an eight.

"If you two don't sit down and play poker, I'll notch the both of you and I won't give a damn if they spell your names right or not," Tulsa Jack warned.

Pierce winked at Newcomb, looking at Tulsa Jack. "So, you're still sore from that last poker game we were in, huh? Well, hell. Let's just go rob the bank here in Purcell. That's probably the only way you'll ever get any money."

"Yeah, Tulsa Jack. Tell you what. Let's go ask that marshal down there which establishment is the best and would he mind if we stole a few dollars and rode off."

Black-Faced Charley was staring at the marshal. His eyes were glazed over. "Let's just kill him and take the whole damn town."

It was about that time that Bitter Creek and Pierce realized their joking with Tulsa Jack was being taken seriously by Black-Faced Charley. At that moment, I was hoping the saloon would burn down or a twister would come through or I could come up with some kind of excuse not to be sitting at that poker table at that moment.

Bitter Creek looked at Black-Faced Charley. "Wait a minute, old hoss. Bob told us not to get into any trouble before we got to the Turkey Track."

"What damn difference does it make?" Black-Faced Charley lamented. "By the time these damn Boomers get done with it, there won't be no Turkey Track or any other kind of ranch in the territory."

"Oh, hell, there's plenty of ranches up in the Cherokee Strip that will still be working," Pierce said. "Besides, I heard Bob was a real good planner and wouldn't lead us wrong."

"Daltons, Daltons, Daltons. I heard of a couple of marshals named Dalton," I said, trying to change the subject again.

"Yeah, Frank got killed in a shootout with the Smith-Dixon gang last year and Bob and Grat were made deputy marshals, but I think they've got other plans," Pierce said.

"You look kind of pale, Three-Fingered," I said.

"Don't mention it. I always feel faint when somebody mentions shooting," he answered.

Bitter Creek reached over and slapped him on the back. "Don't you worry none. We won't make you Two-Fingered Jake just yet. As long as you're sitting between me and the marshal, I know I got something to catch any bullets thrown my way."

At that point, Jake tipped over backwards in his chair in a dead faint. That caught the marshal's attention and he wandered over. The four cowboys were as cool as they come.

"What's his problem?" the marshal asked.

I leaned over and looked down at Three-Fingered. "We were discussin' target practice and he just couldn't take it. He looks kind of peaceful for a change."

The marshal noticed all the hardware on the cowboys. "Who's your friends, D.W.?"

"Oh, just some cowboys passin' through. They've been chasin' some cow thieves. There's two Charleys, a George and a Jack," I said. Each one nodded as I pointed them out. "Boys, this here is W.H. Carr, our token lawman in the town."

I could see Deputy Carr was sizing them up, but since they hadn't done anything, he left them alone. "I see you're chasin' Boomers this evenin'. Havin' much luck?"

He snorted. "Yeah. I got more damn fool land owners than I know what to do with. I guess I'll go back down the street and see what's going on elsewhere. Boys."

The "boys" nodded to him. Black-Faced Charley looked like he was about to sink his fangs into the marshal, but resisted the impulse.

I stood up and shook my head, looking down at Jake again. They laughed as I picked up his shoulders and started dragging him out of the building. I stopped for a moment, "It's been entertainin' meetin' you fellas. I think I'd stay in the cowboy business if I were you. The cows don't shoot back."

"Civilization is abroad in this country now, sure. Of late, our town has been visited by insurance, book, fruit tree and lightning-rod agents in profusion. If that does not look like civilization here, we would like to know what does."
                              ... *The Purcell Register, Nov. 10, 1888*

Chapter 4

Come to Oklahoma and stake your claim to a quarter section of land. Oklahoma was being promoted in every paper in the country and a lot of other places in the world. The Unassigned Lands were the last hope of the landless, where the milk and honey flows and fence posts take root and grow.

By mid-April in 1889, you'd have thought that Purcell had suddenly turned into Ft. Worth. Hell's Half Acre in that north Texas town had nothing on Purcell as thousands of people camped out in every available spot and kept the cash registers ringing all along Main Street. The South Canadian River was the southern boundary for the big land grab. Since there were only about ten or so fords across the river, it was pretty effective in holding back the throngs that wanted to get in there a little early to stake a claim.

The Boomers had been busy over the past few months and were trying to bully the newcomers into believing they had some clout. Signs were posted all over town: "Fair warning. Late order made at regular meeting of Oklahoma Legion. Resolved that we protect our brother members in their long respected rights on selected claims, and that all townsite sharks and claim jumpers will be dealt with in a summary manner."

Not a whole lot of people who were waiting for the big shindig to get started could read what was written on the cards, but they sure found out quick those cards were real good for starting fires.

And, horses. You wouldn't believe the horseflesh that was paraded up and down the streets. Every livery barn in town was

29

crowded with the finest animals money could buy. As the land run got closer, the bids on these animals went up. I even had a few offers for L.G., but that land run business was too much like work and L.G. and I never did more than we absolutely had to. I couldn't see putting him in a situation where some fool would beat my poor mule just to get a little bit of land.

This would have been a fine time to be in the whiskey business except that it just wasn't healthy to be running liquor into town. Along with all those deputy marshals, there were troops of cavalry wandering over all creation trying to catch those folks who were slipping into the Oklahoma Eden a few days ahead of schedule.

One morning, thirteen prairie schooners entered the Promised Land at a ford about four miles north of Purcell on the old cattle trail. After a bunch of folks complained to the marshals, a posse headed after the wagons - one marshal per wagon. You could hear the gunfire from miles away. This was a bunch of diehard Texans that weren't about to give up land they'd staked months before. One deputy was wounded and seven of the would-be settlers. They had to spend the day of the run in a stockade built southwest of Purcell to hold the Sooners that got caught.

A day or two before the April 22nd date of Harrison's Hoss Race, Company L of the 5th Cavalry showed up to patrol the northern bank of the South Canadian. One poor soldier boy had to stand on the railroad bridge to keep them land-hungry fools from leaving early.

Eight trains were waiting for the noon signal that would send thousands of folks streaming across those rolling hills. I couldn't wait for all the fuss to pass Purcell by. There were more fakirs and gamblers in town than there were citizens. You couldn't walk down the street without tripping over two or three of them at a time. I couldn't even find a place to set up my faro game.

I decided to sit up on Red Hill and watch the madness. It

was a beautiful day. The river was running a little full since there had been some rain earlier in the week. You could see the soldier boys sitting in the middle of the river watching the crowd at the train station on the other bank. I watched as the first train inched up the tracks to the bridge. The train wouldn't enter the Unassigned Lands until the signal was given.

The horses were dancing at the edge of the water as the excitement of the moment continued to build. Behind the riders were the wagons and buggies and people on foot eager to get to the Promised Land. The wagons had to line up at the fords, but a few people on foot were willing to test the quicksand just to get an advantage over someone else.

Somebody said more than 50,000 people pushed off into the new Oklahoma that day and I swear most of them went through Purcell. I couldn't believe it. All those people were headed off in the wrong direction. They would have been a whole lot happier spending their time playing poker or drinking in a saloon instead of trying to find a place for some chickens to scratch.

Before the day was over, there were brand new towns all up and down the river. Lexington was staked out just across the river from Purcell. Somebody decided that the town on the other side of the railroad bridge should be named for the Secretary of the Interior who started all this mess so Noble was born. Then, up at the next water stop, Norman Switch became the town of Norman. Civilization as we'd never known it was about to begin.

When the shots rang out from the soldiers and marshals along the river, the race was on. There was a roar from the crowd as they urged their animals onward. The train whistles blew from every train setting up a sound that had every hair on the back of my neck standing up and begging for mercy. Even if Moses had been there to part the sea of prairie grass in the face of Pharoah's army, you would not have seen such a horde descending on the land of milk and honey. There wasn't anything waiting for them but a dugout and a bedpot full of dreams.

I watched the fastest horses disappear into the distance while the wagons lumbered along behind. Those folks with the oxen brought up the rear. I felt sorry for some of them. There wasn't enough land out there for everybody who was in this race. Red Hill was crowded on this day with people from all over who came to watch.

"That's the worst deal the Indians have ever gotten," said an Indian wrapped in a blanket that looked vaguely familiar.

"What do you mean?" I asked, watching him slowly sit down next to an old cedar tree.

"Giving away those lands over there to white men who can't take care of it and don't know the first thing about what the land can tell them."

"You sound like some philosopher. You been watchin' this long?"

"There's very little I haven't seen. My father was driven here from Mississippi years ago when he was a boy. Now, it looks like I'll be driven out of my home too."

"That's progress for you," I said. "These here folks are bringin' civilization to the territory. The best the white man has to offer will be available here."

At that point, the middle-aged Indian fell over laughing. "The best the white man has to offer is death, disease and dishonesty. I prefer the lack of civilization that I grew up with."

As he rolled over, I noticed the black blanket had a white buffalo in the middle of it. "Where'd you find that blanket? It's mighty handsome."

"I believe that you left it behind for some railroad workers a few years ago. They figured that they had taken an old Indian by charging me a dollar for the blanket. However, the weave is quite exceptional. You should never have thrown it away like that."

"You seem to know quite a bit about me. I think you've got me at a disadvantage."

"Actually, I have a feeling you are a disadvantage. Oh, well.

I'm George Big Tree. I live out west of town. I believe it's about two miles south of your still."

"Big Tree. Big Tree," I repeated, ignoring his obvious jab at my character. I squinted my eyes trying to place him.

"You know. The large brick house on the south bank of Walnut Creek."

"Oh. That house," I replied. "I don't recall seein' you around very much."

"That's because I learned how to move without being seen. You know, I am the wind in the night, the rustle of grass, the quiet of the wolf. Just because I'm named Big Tree doesn't mean I thrash around when I'm on the prowl."

"Right. And I suppose you can track a coyote over bare rock in a dust storm, too."

"Well, I haven't tried that, but I reckon that is entirely within the scope of my natural abilities."

Now it was my turn to laugh. "So, you like my old blanket."

"No, I like my blanket," he said as he loosened the blanket while he leaned against the tree.

"You sound pretty well educated for an Indian."

"I am very well educated as a member of one of the Five Civilized Tribes. I've attended some of the best schools the East has to offer. The missionaries thought they saw something of value in me and decided to further my education in far distant places. I am a Chickasaw, in case you were wondering."

"How'd you get a name like George, then?"

"Even as a boy I was inclined to always tell the truth, no matter how much it might hurt. The missionaries thought they were honoring me by naming me after your first president. George Washington, I think his name was."

"You sure do have a sharp tongue."

"Better sharp than forked, as they say."

"So why're you sittin' on top of Red Hill instead of behind some desk somewhere? You'd make a great politician."

"Well, it just so happens that I've spent the past year in

Washington, D.C., trying to prevent this spectacle we're witnessing today. Seeing how badly all my efforts have fared, I thought I'd come here in an outfit in which no one would recognize me."

"Maybe I ought to just call one of them New York newspapermen over here and have them talk to you."

"You don't want to do that. Then I'll have to tell them you are the largest supplier of illegal alcohol in the Indian Territory."

I started laughing. "If you knew that, why haven't you told someone who could do somethin' about it?"

"Ah. One of the aspects of living in a white man's world is having access to a white man's liquor supply. All of those official meetings in your nation's capitol start with a round of drinks and end with a round of drinks. I've grown accustomed to imbibing spirits on a regular basis. Unfortunately, I have found your particular brand of poison to be one of the best tasting anywhere around. As soon as I figure out what your secret ingredient is, I'll have them arrest you and make my own," he said, his black eyes dancing with laughter.

"You folks lost Georgia, Alabama, Mississippi, Florida, the Dakotas, Colorado, Kansas, Nebraska. Hell, you've lost 'em all. What makes you think you could hold on to this little piece of Eden?"

"Eden?" he said, snickering. "After all the Indians that have died in this forsaken place in the middle of nowhere, you still call it Eden. Unfortunately, there is nothing else left. And, I for one, would like to keep one bit of open range for the Indians."

"Even if you could manage that, it'd never last. They've been huntin' gold and silver in the Wichita Mountains since the Spaniards first came through. It'd be just like the Black Hills. You couldn't stand up to the cavalry then, and you can't now," I said with a somewhat holier-than-thou attitude.

"You may be right. But, just once, I'd like the United States government to live up to just one of its treaties. Just for the sake of one Indian child." He shook his head. "Look, the dust has settled and you can't even tell there were thousands of white men standing on this side of the river an hour ago. They disappeared like rattlesnakes down prairie dog holes. And, they are just as dangerous."

I reached into my saddlebag and pulled out a bottle with a clear, brownish liquid in it. "Here, George, this one's on me. Let's drink a toast to a world that doesn't look anythin' like the one we'd like."

George sat up and took the bottle. He peered through the liquid at the land across the river. "Here's to a land that brought alive the challenge of living and that will be no more."

He took a long, slow pull on the bottle. He chuckled, "Those folks don't know what they've gotten into. I read those newspapers back East describing this land. You couldn't tell it was the same piece of ground. After a few of those tornadoes and a couple of those long, dry spells, these folks will wonder why in the world they left their homes in the first place."

"They were lookin' for somethin' better. All those problems over the horizon can't hurt you a bit. It's only when you catch up with them that you start to worry."

"How much did you really make off those railroaders? There's now a legend about a gambler and an Indian chief whose ghosts you can see running across the Canadian River bottom on moonlit nights when the sound of a train whistle rouses them from their slumber in a bed of quicksand."

"Really, I missed that tale."

"You have to ride the rails and listen to the trainmen as they pull into the station. Now, how much?"

"Oh, about four hundred dollars."

"Good. I'm always glad to see the railroad come out on the short end of anything. I could probably find a couple of those fellows for you, if you'd like to try again. I'll even give you your blanket back."

"No. That's quite all right. If there's one thin' I have learned over the years, it's not to unbury any unwanted memories of losses of property that was dear to you. Them railroaders never have had much of a sense of humor."

"The plague of locusts they have brought upon the land will never be silenced," Big Tree said, obviously feeling the effects of the libation.

"Maybe you should have been a preacher. You could talk to them sinners plain, you know, one heathen to another," I snickered.

"No. I should have been a renegade Indian, scalping unwary white men as they wandered across the prairies. As a matter of fact, perhaps I should start now with you."

"Now, why in hell would you want to do that? I haven't done anything bad to you that I can recall."

"I had an uncle once. Broken Foot. He was a hunter. Loved to chase buffalo, deer, turkey. Any kind of game. He could track a coyote across solid rock. He always used to tell me about this funny white man who always brought around a jug and got him drunk just about the time the Indian agent paid a visit. This white man never missed. The only thing wrong with Broken Foot, other than his penchant for whiskey, was that his foot was badly twisted and he couldn't run. He was tracking some old mama bear, one of the last in this country, when she took out after him. His gun jammed and that old mama bear made tracks up his back that even you could have followed. I don't know that he died particularly happy, but at least he was doing what he enjoyed."

"I seem to remember a Chickasaw named Broken Foot."

"You should. That's where I learned to appreciate your whiskey. The two of you would get drunk. The Indian agent would come and look disgusted at the two of you. You would spend the next twenty minutes trying to get him to put you on the dole. It must have been that pasty white face and scraggly brown hair of yours that gave you away."

"So, that's why you want to scalp me."

"Not at all. I want to get even with you for all the tricks you've played on other white men by pretending to be Indian."

"I thought you liked that," I said with a puzzled look on my face.

"I don't care what you do to other white men, but you keep giving Indians a bad name," he replied.

"Go to the Fashion Saloon at Lexington, Ok Territory for pure wines and liquors for medical purposes."
... The Purcell Register, Oct. 18, 1890

Chapter 5

Perched high on the bluff overlooking the South Canadian River, the denizens of Purcell and the Chickasaw Nation could look eastward across the riverbed to Lexington. Most people saw two rival towns in a raw land. I, of course, saw opportunity. Purcell was dry and thirsty. Lexington flowed with the pure spirits that could slake the cravings of the driest souls in the territory.

Lexington, O.T., was named after a much more famous Lexington in Kentucky. Following in the footsteps of its more famous predecessor, the Lexington in the territory had the largest number of distilleries in business anywhere in Oklahoma. There wasn't a single street in town that didn't have two or three saloons doing business of one sort or another. These legal stills damn near put me out of business, but my secret ingredient kept bartenders on both sides of the river asking for more.

I was sitting up on the top of Red Hill one afternoon, listening to the singing coming from the Catholic school a short ways away when I noticed a steady stream of individuals hiking across the riverbed to Lexington and an unsteady stream of those same individuals weaving back across the river. That trail was well worn even though the new town was only a month or so old. Then, like a vision from heaven, it struck me. What those folks needed was a business willing to extend itself to even greater lengths to satisfy their needs. By meeting our clients halfway, like in the middle of the river, we could make it easier for them to partake of our brand of liquid refreshment.

Now, I was loaded with the idea, a handy supply of cheap whiskey and a great location. What I needed was a partner or two to put up the stakes in what had to be a sure bet. I knew

38

exactly where to go. This time of day, I was sure to find Robert Wilder at the Clifton House trying to drum up a poker game with the well-heeled travelers that came through Purcell. Sure enough, there he sat, a wild card waiting to be played.

Robert had drifted through Arkansas and Texas before he followed the cattle drives north into the territory. The dust and bad food that came with the cattle drives was more than he was willing to put up with. The first time he laid eyes on the saloons in Kansas and the fancy-pants gamblers, he knew what he would like to do for the rest of his life.

Standing about five-foot, ten-inches tall, he was whipcord lean. His long, thin fingers could whirl a deck of cards around a table faster than any man I ever saw. He loved those fancy vests and a black suit. He liked his felt hat from his cowboying days and wore it with a silver band around the crown. The one thing I like most about Robert was that he had the same thing on his mind that I had on mine - making a buck. And, he sure didn't want to make his money from the topside of no swayback horse.

"Robert, old friend," I said as I walked up to the table where he was playing a game of solitaire. He glared up at me from under the brim of his black Stetson hat. His handlebar mustache drooped down either side of his mouth as he tried his damndest to ignore me. He worked his jaw a couple of times and then turned and shot a stream of brown liquid at the closest spittoon.

"What kind of a con game are you running this time?" he accused.

"Con game? Me? Not on your life. I have seen the errors of my ways and have gone straight."

He laughed, "The only way you'll go straight is to hell. You're ruining any chance I have of working up a game this afternoon."

"I've got a business proposition that I know you'll like," I told him with my most persuasive tone of voice. "This is a sure-fire way to make a killin'."

"You keep bothering me and your killing will come a little

sooner than you're expecting." He leaned back in his chair and gazed at me with those gray eyes of his. "The only thing sure-fire about your plans is that they lose money."

"That's why I need a partner who can handle the money and run the business." I glanced around to make sure no one was within spitting distance. "Have you noticed how much saloon business has been goin' across the river lately?"

"I sure as hell wouldn't be sitting here talking to you if there was any action here."

"Right. Now, I have the perfect location for a saloon that will make sure we can draw a crowd. I can guarantee you that this location will become the hottest spot in the territory." I emphasized my point by tapping my finger forcibly on the table in front of him.

"All right, Mr. Genius, where is this place that's so hot?"

"In the middle of the South Canadian River."

He snorted so hard when he heard that, tobacco juice came spurting out his nose. He sucked his breath back in and some of that tobacco juice went right down his windpipe. He started choking and coughing and I was almost afraid I was going to lose a partner before he even had a chance to say no. I reached over and pounded him on his back as he spit his wad of tobacco all over the table and floor. Gasping for breath, he wheezed, "Are you crazy?"

"Not at all. Think about it. There is a trail across the river bottom from Purcell to Lexington and it is well worn," I said pointing off towards the river. "Let's build a saloon right across the middle of that trail as close to the water's edge as we can get it. We'd still be in Oklahoma Territory and we'd be the first place a thirsty man from Indian Territory could stop and get a legal drink. We could call it Heaven's Gate Saloon. You know, offer the finest sippin' whiskey as a little taste of heaven before those poor souls have to cross the river to those dry environs. There's a lot more people livin' in Purcell than in Lexington. Everyone in the northern half of the Chickasaw Nation comes through here at one time or another. Hell, we could organize wagon rides from the hotels to the saloons. We could drive 'em right out to the saloon so our patrons wouldn't have to get their feet wet."

I paused for a moment to catch my breath and see if Robert had caught up to his. The more I talked about the saloon the bigger and grander it became. I was surprised at how excited I felt.

"You damn near make sense," he said, with his face a bright red and tears streaming down his face. "That's bad when you make sense. I know I'm going to regret this, but, what's it going to take?"

"We'd need a two-story building with the saloon and gambling tables downstairs and couple of extra work rooms upstairs. You can pick the games and run the tables. I'll work the bar and brew a little John Barleycorn and in no time at all they'll be lined up just waitin' to give us their money."

With his face returning to its normal taciturn expression, Robert reached out across the table and grabbed the lapel of my coat. "What would make me think I could trust you as far as I could throw you?"

"You've already noted that my success in business has been less than inspirin'. However, I could see from the top of Red Hill that this could work. I've got a little money saved up from my whiskey business and I'll throw that in just to prove I'm serious."

Robert let go of my coat and let me flop back down in my chair. He got up and walked to the door of the saloon and looked down the Main Street of Purcell. Even at this time of day he could see that a lot of folks were headed for the river. Of course, the train station was down there, too, but I didn't mention that. He walked slowly back, to the table and reached across with his right hand. "When do we start?"

"Right now, partner," I said as I pumped his hand excitedly.

Before the sun set on the Indian Territory the next day, we

were the talk of the town. All the prim and proper ladies avoided us on the street - of course they already avoided me. But now, they pointed at us with their gloved hands from behind parasols and packages.

The biggest ruckus was raised in Lexington when the workers went out and started throwing up the framework. The usual line of customers had to detour around the construction and complained bitterly that we were making them go an extra distance to get to their whiskey. I kept telling them that we were just about to make it a whole lot easier for them.

The Heaven's Gate Saloon was just about my first and last chance at breaking out of my humdrum life. I didn't have any more money and I was down to my last good idea. The part of Oklahoma Territory where the land run was held was being governed by the rules of the Nebraska Territory. One of those rules was that alcohol could only be sold for medicinal purposes. I knew I had a way to handle this. I headed for the Pottawatomie country where Linc was running a pharmacy.

He was now a full-time people doctor and he was getting a little snooty for my purposes. But, I needed him. They must have seen me coming because by the time I got to his store, the door was closed and the sign said, "The Doctor Is Out." Well, as far as needing a doctor, he could stay out for all I cared. I wasn't about to use him for no doctor considering how many of my horses had died under his medical guidance. But, he was real key to us getting that saloon up and running as quickly as possible.

I got off my horse and tied the reins to the hitching post out front. I walked up the front steps and peered through the window to see where they were. I knocked on the door real good and shouted, "Lincoln, I need to talk to you."

A voice from the back room said, "Go away. I ain't interested."

I could tell by the way this conversation was starting that it might take a little bit more effort to convince him this was a serious matter. "I've got a business proposition for you."

"I told you once and I'll tell you again, I'm not interested in any more of your hare-brained schemes."

"I've got a business in Purcell, uh, Lexington, uh, over yonder that could make the two of us some serious money, but I need your help."

Linc finally walked out of the back room and stared at me through the window. He didn't open the door though.

"Look, D.W., I have put a lot of time and effort into my doctoring people and I don't want to backslide by getting bamboozled into another one of your dodges."

"Not this time, Linc. I've got a business partner over in Purcell and we're puttin' up this establishment over there that has the potential to make a lot of money. But . . . "

"But, but, but. There's always a but with you and it's my butt that usually gets caught in the bear trap."

"This time, though, you don't have to do anythin' that's agin the law. As a matter of fact, we need your doctorin' expertise in our business."

His eyes narrowed as he stared at me trying to figure out if I was telling the truth or not. I could tell he didn't believe what he was hearing, but I had him interested now. He opened the door and let me come inside. He glanced out the window, up and down the street to make sure no one had seen me. After leading me to the back room, he pulled the curtain across the door.

"All right, now what do you want?"

"I've got a legitimate business bein' built over in Purcell even as we speak. But, me and my partner need your services to make our business a goin' concern."

"Who in their right mind would go into business with you?"

"Robert Wilder."

"The gambler?"

"Of course the gambler. How else do you expect a saloon to get any business without some gamblers?"

"I always did doubt his sanity. Now, I'm sure he doesn't

have a lick of sense. He could have done better than ending up with you, D.W."

"Now, Linc, this here is a real good way for you to make some money without doin' much in the way of work. All you have to do is sit at the front door and write prescriptions for our customers. Charge 'em two bits apiece for your name on a piece of paper that says our customer is there to get alcohol for medicinal purposes. How much easier can it get? And, this is legitimate."

"Hell, it can't be too legitimate if you're selling whiskey over the counter in Purcell. Indian Territory is dry now and probably always will be. You know them Indians can't hold their liquor."

"Well, it's not exactly in Purcell."

"Even if it's in Lexington, you got more saloons there than you can shake a stick at. What makes you think you're so damn special?"

"Well, it's not exactly in Lexington."

"Then, where in the hell is it?"

"Well," I said, pursing my lips as I waited for his response, "it's kinda halfway between Purcell and Lexington."

"There ain't nothing between Purcell and Lexington except that dad-blamed river."

It took a moment for that statement to sink into his brain. I looked around his new office admiring his fancy new table and all those shiny tools he had on the table near the wall.

"You can't be serious? Have you gone completely mad? You can't build a saloon in the middle of the river!"

"Why not? It's perfect. Most of the saloon business that ends up in Lexington comes from Purcell. You ought to see the trail they've beat across that riverbed. You know there's a good ford there and no quicksand. All we're doin' is buildin' our saloon right across that path. All those thirsty cowhands and merchants and train passengers will see us first. It's like a royal flush sittin' on the bank of the South Canadian River. It can't miss."

"Of course it can miss. You're involved in it."

"Now, Linc, that's why I've got Robert as a partner. He takes care of the business side of the saloon and the gamblin'. I take care of the whiskey and bar. We bring in a madam and a couple of girls and we've struck gold in that there sand box."

"Oh, Lord, this does sound like a good idea. Oh, Lord, somebody else must have thought this up. Oh, Lord, I know I'm in trouble when one of your ideas sounds good."

"Hmm, I think I've heard that somewhere else before. Look, Linc, all you have to do is sit at the front door, examine each patient as they come through the door and fill out those prescriptions so these poor, sick folks can find their medicinal relief from the maladies of livin' in a dry territory. You can be there any time you want, exceptin' we will need you a lot on Friday and Saturday nights. You can write one prescription per drink or one prescription per person. Hell, you've run a drug store here and in Kansas so you know how to fill out the forms. It won't take much effort and you can include us in your weekly rounds. This is a chance for you to expand your medical practice while it makes us the only legal saloon in the Oklahoma Territory."

He sat there wrestling with the proposition. I could tell he had a million reasons why he shouldn't do it, but the almighty dollar kept him from listening to any one reason.

"All right. I'll give it a shot. But I don't want any more of your shenanigans."

"Done, Brother. You won't regret this in the least."

"That's what you said the last time and the time before that and the time before that, and so on," he said. "I should know better than to listen to you, even when you make sense."

"You won't regret this Linc. You will have a ton of men folks in this part of the country just waitin' for your tender ministrations."

"Fred Ferry is building a boat on the Lexington side of the river and will build on it a saloon. When this is completed, can we not claim that we have a Ferry boat?"

. . . The Purcell Register, Oct. 25, 1890

Chapter 6

Not many saloons have been built in the middle of a riverbed, but that's where the Heaven's Gate Saloon opened for business. No sooner did we start on our saloon than another seedy type started building one next door. He called his establishment the Sand Bar Saloon. Obviously, the man had no imagination. However, he did like to sell whiskey. Competition started real fast when he began selling drinks off of a couple of boards set up across some sawhorses.

Not to be outdone, we promptly brought in a cook and offered up some fine Oklahoma Territory vittles for our customers. We put our door across a couple of empty kegs and started up a poker game on the sand outside the saloon while the workers finished off the inside. Unfortunately, that idea didn't last too long in those twenty-mile-per-hour winds that scattered the cards and folding money from here to White Bead Hill. We finally had to postpone the gaming until the walls were up and caulked.

We let the city marshal know that one of the saloons in Sand Bar Town was doing business illegally, but he didn't seem to care one way or tother. We were outside the city limits and the riverbed was federal territory. The federal marshals had bigger fish to fry with all the outlaws roaming the territory.

So, that left us with our biggest hole card - the upstairs portion of our business. In a territory with a lot of unmarried cowhands and outlaws on the run, there was a prime opportunity to run a profit by providing pleasures of the flesh to those poor, lonely young lads. Well, by the time we were done with them, they'd be poor anyhow.

We generally didn't open the saloon until mid-afternoon since morning business wasn't worth the effort. Robert and I were standing on the sidewalk at the top of Depot Hill in Purcell when a stagecoach from Tahlequah pulled up. You see, all the railroads ran from north to south across the territory. Not a one ran from east to west.

We could tell a ruckus was brewing when the driver unceremoniously dumped a carpetbag off the top of the coach and into the middle of the street. He jumped down and yanked open the coach door.

"Git yore ass outta there," he bellowed at someone inside.

"I paid for a ticket to Tucson. I'll be damned if I'm setting one foot outside this coach," came back an answer from a throaty voice.

"I've had all the foul-mouthed language I can take from a skirt. You can git yore money back from the agent. But you are comin' out of that coach right now. You can either step out or I'll drag yore sorry ass outta there."

Reaching into the coach, he grabbed the woman's arm and started to pull her out. A booted foot came flying out the door, catching the man on his chin. He yelled and dropped his hold on her, looking around for something to use to hit her with. A string of curses came pouring out of the coach interspersed with orders for the driver to put her bag back on the coach and to get a move on.

Cursing under his breath, the driver reached up into the boot of the coach and pulled out an old sawed-off shotgun. He cracked the gun open to check the load, clicked it back together and went around to the far side of the coach. Throwing open the door, he pointed the shotgun at the woman and said, in no uncertain terms, that he hadn't ever shot a woman before but she was about to end that here and now. He told her to get out of the coach before he blew her out.

"Well, I never in my life . . .," she huffed as she looked at the driver.

She was cut short in her latest tirade by the sound of the shotgun being cocked. Everyone on Main Street had stopped to watch this little melodrama unfold. You could have heard a pin drop except for the steady stream of cuss words that came from the coach. Both Robert and I stared with interest to see what kind of woman this was going to be. Neither one of us was prepared for what emerged. With a throaty voice like that, we expected a hefty woman to step down from the coach. Instead, a woman of medium height and slim build gazed out the window of the coach at the Main Street of Purcell. At the continued urging of the driver, she alighted in the street.

Her dark hair was pinned up under a hat that was slightly askew on the left side of her head. She had a narrow, thin face with prominent cheekbones. The bright red lipstick she wore provided a contrast to brilliant blue eyes that were literally shooting sparks. She wore a blue taffeta fancy dress with a bright sash and gewgaws all up and down the front.

Robert wasted no time in walking up to her. "Howdy, ma'am. Can I be of assistance?" he asked as he swept his hat off his head and bowed.

She glared at him as though he was the last man she ever wanted to meet. From that look on her face, she would have shot him if she'd had a gun handy. "Where in the name of hell's half-acre am I?"

"Why the Queen City of the Chickasaw Nation, of course," he replied, ignoring her expression. "You've landed on your feet in Purcell, Indian Territory."

"Great. Just great," she muttered. "I was hoping I could at least clear this godforsaken stretch of nowhere."

"My name's Robert Wilder and this is my partner, D.W. Sweden," he said, waving towards me. His glance never left her face. "I didn't catch your name."

She looked me up and down, the left corner of her mouth turned up in a sneer. "Is this supposed to be my welcoming committee? If so, you fall damned well short of my wants and desires."

I just kind of laughed at that. "If it had been left up to that stagecoach driver, Mr. Buck Shot would have welcomed you personally."

The loud commotion of the woman being dumped in the street had attracted a crowd. Some of the fine ladies of the town were standing around with their noses out of joint, sniffing judiciously in her direction. Seeing the unwanted attention, Robert reached down and picked up the woman's bag - which is more than I would have done - and touched her elbow to guide her towards the Compton Hotel.

"Who in the hell told you to adopt me?" she said vehemently through clenched teeth, wrenching her arm out of his grip. "Just let me find another stage line and you won't see me for my dust."

With a somewhat roguish grin, he said, "You know, you're just what this town needs. A wildcat in woman's clothing. My partner and I have a proposition for you."

She narrowed her eyes as she appraised him and then me. I started to protest my lack of enthusiasm for having her around, but Robert shot a warning look in my direction.

"Now why were you headed for Tucson?" Robert asked.

The fire came back into her eyes and voice. "How in the hell did you know that?"

"We could hear your dainty voice half way down the street."

"Oh," she replied. "Well. Hmmmm. I was on my way to work for a friend of mine."

"Where?"

"At a business there."

"What kind of business?"

"A saloon, is that what you wanted to hear, you fancified excuse for a gentleman?"

"I thought so," Robert said, with another warning glare at me. "You don't have to go to Arizona to find work in an up and coming saloon. We've got one right here and we can probably offer you a much better deal."

She put her hands on her hips and looked up and down the street at the two or three saloons in sight. "Which one is it?"

"Why none of these," Robert laughed. "This is Indian Territory and it's dry. You have to go across the river into Oklahoma Territory to buy any liquor legally."

"So, you've got a place in that town over there," she said, pointing to the east.

I just stood there and shook my head. For some reason, I already knew where this conversation was going.

"Well, not exactly."

"Where? Exactly."

Robert gazed at me and then back at her. "In the middle of the riverbed."

"Are you crazy? What kind of damn fool would come up with an idea to put a saloon in the middle of the river?"

I knew I'd heard this conversation before. Robert pointed to me.

"Oh, great," she said. "This overblown dirt farmer comes up with a crazy idea, you believe him and you want me to work there. Forget it."

"Wait. Hear us out."

"Just wait till I get my hands on that jitney driver. I'll tear his liver out and feed it to the dogs," she muttered as she stood in the middle of the boardwalk, shaking her head back and forth.

Obviously, Robert wasn't going to be discouraged so easily. I was beginning to think that he really was befuddled.

"At least let us buy you lunch and you can listen to our proposal. That can't hurt," he said. "There's not another stage out of here until tomorrow and the southbound train doesn't come through here until later this afternoon."

At the mention of a free meal, her head swung around. "Free food, huh?"

"With all the trimmin's," I said with a less-than-enthusiastic smile.

She eyed me up and down, then sniffed loudly. I was kind
of insulted since I had on my Sunday-go-to-meeting clothes with
my black coat and dark brown pants. I even had a clean white
shirt on. She must not have liked my sweat-soaked dark gray
hat. She sure couldn't have minded what I smelled like because
I had just put on some toilet water that morning.

Grabbing Robert's arm, she said, "Lead on."

We went into the hotel lobby and headed for the dining
room. A half-dozen tables were in the room, but only a couple
of them were being put to good use. I ended up with the job of
lugging her carpetbag into the hotel. I don't know what she was
taking to Tucson, but it felt like her bustle was full of rocks.
Robert had his come-hither smile on his face doing his best to
charm her out of her bloomers. I hoped he would because we
needed a caboose like hers to bring up the rear of our success-
bound train.

When they reached the table, Robert had to wrestle her for
the chair. Finally, she let him pull it out while she eased down
into the seat. He beamed at her as he continued his palaver
while sitting facing her. I dropped the bag in an empty chair and
straddled the fourth chair.

"D.W., this is Sandra Peaks," Robert said.

I raised my eyebrows at this bit of news. He had finally gotten something out of her besides a hard time.

"You can call me Sandy, for short," she said, nodding at me.

"Since your Peaks are Sandy, does that mean your valleys are
Sandy, too," I replied, guffawing at my own humor. Robert
glared at me and I rolled my eyes heavenward, looking as con-
trite as I possibly could after hearing a moniker like that.

She must have had some kind of a sense of humor since my
jest didn't seem to phase her a bit. For being a wisp of a woman,
Sandy could put a full-grown man to shame when it came to eating. She must have had two hollow legs and a bottomless stomach. I have never seen a woman put away the food like she did
- steak, potatoes, poke salad, carrots, beans, cornbread, coffee

and pie. She wolfed that food down like a starving coyote in a chicken coop. She didn't even slow down to breathe. I thought I could eat fast, but I would have gone hungry at the hog trough if I'd been sitting next to her. When she finally leaned back in her chair and let out a contented sigh, I thought for sure she'd split a gusset.

"Shore looks like you haven't eaten in awhile," I said.

"Stagecoaches ruin my appetite," she replied. "I can't get that damned dirt out of my mouth and it bothers me when I eat."

Robert and I were both taken aback by her language, but at the same time, we could see that her rough edges did nothing to hide the gem of a woman sitting at the table.

"We just opened the saloon," Robert said. "Our business day usually starts at four o'clock and runs until well after midnight. We've got a blackjack table, a faro board, a roulette wheel and three poker tables. We give them a little something to eat with their gambling and boozing. We're usually full to the brim, but we could stand a little more business. There's another saloon next door that's started to take some customers away, so we need a little added attraction. That's you."

I jumped in, "I make most of our whiskey and it tastes a lot better than your run-of-the-mill firewater. There's three or four distilleries over across the river in Lexington, so we buy some of the better whiskey for those that want to pay more. We don't water our stuff down, too much, so the real hardcases are steady customers."

"We're the only saloon in Sand Bar Town with an upstairs with a couple of rooms. But, we need someone to manage the entertainment," Robert explained. "Seeing that you seem to have some experience in that area, we figured you might want to take it on."

Not being one to beat around the bush, she got right to the point, "What's in it for me?"

I tapped Robert on the shoulder and leaned over so we could

whisper to each other. "I think I have a way to work this so we can all come out with some money if this works the way I think it will."

"It's your crazy idea, again," he replied.

"All right, missy, here's the deal. I run the bar and keep the patrons well juiced up. Robert runs the games and makes sure that we keep our players honest. I make most of my money from the bar while he gets most of his money from the games. Whichever one of us works the hardest makes the most. Here's my proposal. We each operate separately. I keep half of what I make on the bar and give each of you a quarter of my profits. Robert does the same. He keeps half of his profits from the games and you and I get a quarter each. Then, you keep half of what you make from the entertainment and give Robert and me each a quarter. Since Robert put up most of the money to build the place, we'll pay him a set amount each week until the building's paid for. Then, it's clear sailin.' We'll have a good idea of how much business each other is doin' so there won't be any skimmin.' Then, the harder each of us works, the more we all make."

Robert's eyes sort of glazed over as he thought about that split. He had always told me he could make a bunch of money on the tables, but he didn't know how much I was profiting from cooking my own booze. Sandy, of course, was the stickler.

"Neither one of you is putting your ass on the line, so to speak, to make this here little operation successful," she said. "I think I deserve a little more."

"Honey, you can bring in as many girls as you want. If we have to build another crib, by Gen. Joseph Hooker, we will," I said.

"I don't trust either one of you."

Robert looked at me, expecting some words of wisdom, I guess. Where he was going to find them, I had no idea. But, I tried anyway. "Look. We've got the business started. It's a lot nicer climate here than it is in Tucson. There's a steady stream of customers. This is the promised land. I doubt seriously that your friend in Arizona would cut you in on the profits. Most likely, he'd have paid you a weekly wage and kept you hoppin' faster than a one-legged square dancer. We're not askin' you to put any money up. Hell, we ain't even asked if the sheriff was chasin' you. If one is though, you've come to the right place. Every outlaw from Kansas to Texas comes through here. Nights out on that river can get pretty wild."

"I can handle myself," she spat out at me.

"Just like you handled that stagecoach driver?" I spat back.

"You can't win them all," she snapped.

"I don't know Robert. Maybe we should let this one keep on goin'."

Robert pursed his lips and nodded his head.

"Now, wait a minute you two. I didn't say I wouldn't give this some thought."

About that time, a steam whistle echoed down the valley.

"Well, there's your train. I guess I'll help you down to the station," I said.

"What's your hurry? I was just getting comfortable. And, besides, my meal hasn't worn off yet." With a mischievous grin, she said, "Why don't you show me your place? I can probably afford another day in this town. I'll come by and watch your customers this evening and make up my mind."

Robert and I stood up and shook hands. He grabbed her right arm and I grabbed her left arm and we lifted her out of her chair. "That's all we needed to hear," he said.

"An ounce of lead is not very heavy, but if it strikes you just right you cannot carry it."
　　　　　　　　　　. . . *The Purcell Register, Dec. 31, 1887*

Chapter 7

Saturday night in the territory was always a wild time, but Sand Bar Town must have set some kind of record. Since the city marshals left us alone, the one law enforcement we had was W.H. Carr, the deputy U.S. marshal in Purcell. However, he had a lot of territory to cover and was rarely around when trouble broke out. I kept my double-barreled shotgun handy just in case somebody got a little too rowdy.

Linc had settled into the routine and had a special chair built for himself. The chair was at the end of the bar closest to the door under a sign, that read, "The doctor is in," when he was holding court. He liked the money he was making from the prescriptions. I didn't though. I had to give my customers a twenty-five cent discount on their first drink just to keep them happy.

My brother, the doctor, also had a lucrative side business going. He got paid to practice medicine on all those poor souls whose hides were perforated with knives and bullets. As a matter of fact, we kept a collection of used bullets on a shelf behind the bar. We took special pains to point out to some of our newer customers than not everyone was lucky in cards, love or gunfights.

We had one bullet with a satin ribbon tied around it to mark Sandy's contribution to the memorial. Seems like she took a fellow upstairs and was just settling him into bed when a bullet came whizzing through the floor and lodged in the guy's backside. He came roaring out of that room with his long johns flapping in the breeze. Sandy came chasing him down the stairs with her bloomers in one hand and a surprised look on her face, trying to figure out what happened. He stopped long enough to bend over and point to his obvious source of discomfort.

55

"Is that all that's wrong with you? I ought to take a gun and shoot you where it really hurts. You're just trying to skip out of paying your bill."

"Bill, hell," he snorted. "You'll be damned lucky if I don't shoot you in the butt, too."

She flounced over to the bar with her drawers hanging out. Every eye in the place was glued to her scantily clad figure, hoping a button would fly loose or a strap would break.

"D.W.," she screamed. "Where in the hell is that worthless doctor you call a brother? Get his behind in here so he can work on this guy's behind. I haven't got time to waste on non-paying customers."

That was Sandy. Always ready and willing to share her womanly charms and social graces. Of course, she was a little peeved that nobody else had yet stepped up to take this guy's place.

Linc, hearing the commotion, walked in the front door. He went to his chair and picked up his medical bag. With his bowler hat at a jaunty angle on his head, he sauntered over to the guy who had been shot. He told the poor fellow to bend over the table and grit his teeth. Nodding to Sandy, he said, "Madame, I would be more than happy to assist you. Which cheek did you say he forgot to turn?"

She stormed off upstairs to put her clothes back on while Linc went to work.

"That looks a little nasty. I don't think you'll be sitting down very much over the next few days. I hope you can ride standing up. That'll be five dollars up front," Linc said.

The man wasn't about to argue with the only doctor in the saloon. You could see by the expression on his face that he was in considerable pain. By the time, they got the fellow settled down and the blood washed off, all Linc had to do was reach down with his fingers and pluck the bullet out of the guy's hind end. The bullet had come through the floor at an angle and caught part of the mattress, which slowed the bullet down enough so that it didn't go too deep. It did take Linc a little time to clean the wound and pluck all the feathers out though.

After that, we posted a poetic notice on the wall:

"If you're going to shoot your pistol, take aim at wall or floor.

This rule you've got to follow or you can't come here no more.

You must be a little careful when you enter our front door.

If you aim your pistol skyward, you could perforate a whore.

Sandy didn't appreciate our use of a certain word, but it was the only one we could think of that rhymed. Besides, it was effective in cutting down on holes in the ceiling and the upstairs customers. Although, there seemed to be a lot more foot injuries in later days.

Shortly after opening the Heaven's Gate Saloon, we found that staying in one piece on a Saturday night was a major problem. Getting the money from the saloon to the bank the next day without getting a few bullet holes was a major cause for celebration.

It wasn't long before I traded my nice oak bar for a stack of railroad ties with an oak top. You'd be amazed at how many bullets a good railroad tie could stop. Robert and I had worked out a way to cover the door should anyone feel like relieving us of our nightly take.

The first Saturday night of the month was the one where we had to hire an extra guard or two to keep the order. The cowboys were the wildest and Sandy's three girls hardly ever got to take a break. By this time, Sandy spent most of her time down in the bar watching Robert deal cards. She kept track of the girls and collected the money before the cowboys went upstairs. Since we only had two rooms upstairs, she kept a steady rotation going all night long. If that woman had been in charge of Sherman's march through Georgia, they could have made enough money to buy Canada and Mexico.

One particular Saturday afternoon, though, we were visited by a deputy marshal. As I was standing behind the bar polishing glasses, Deputy Carr strolled in. Business was slow and only a handful of customers were lounging around. It was a cold day in early November. The late afternoon sun's rays were streaming in through the window, warming up the bar. It was a lazy kind of a day and I knew that night would be a wild one, so I was hoping the marshal would stick around.

The deputy leaned against the bar and cast a jaundiced eye over everyone in the saloon. Without turning his back to anyone in the room, he asked me, "All right, D.W., what kind of no good are you up to now?"

"Me? This is the first honest business I've had in years. I've never worked so hard in my life. Look at these hands. Rough, red. Hell, the knuckles are damn near bleedin'."

Pointing to one of our customers, he said, "Who's that funny looking fellow? He looks awful suspicious."

"Why that's ol' Skunkbit. He's kinda harmless. He looks a whole lot meaner than he really is. He don't take his hat off to no man nor woman nor even in church. Come to think of it, though, I can't ever recall him bein' in church," I noted.

"Still seems mighty peculiar. How'd he get that way?"

"Well, a rabid skunk was a'chasin' him across the pasture and he climbed a tree. Only problem was that the tree was a mite small. He went so high up in that little tree that it bent plumb over to the ground. That ol' skunk was close enough by then to take a nip out of his ear. You could hear his scream for miles around. He shinnied back down that tree, or up if you will, till it sprung up again. Knowin' he was bit, he took out his knife and sliced his ear off. Kinda messy, but he didn't come down with no foamin' mouth. That's why he wears that cap of his down so low on the left side. Somebody said he cut up an old man that tried to take that cap off," I explained, shrugging my shoulders. "Skunkbit just kinda fits him. I can't recall his last name. I don't think I ever heard anybody call him anythin' but

Skunkbit."

"Hmph. Well, enough of that. I came looking for someone with the same last name as yours. You know a Linc Sweden?"

"Shore do."

"Is he any kin?"

"Uh-huh."

"What's he to you?"

"My older brother."

"I hear tell he's a doctor in these parts."

"He's been known to fix a few folks up," I said, wondering where this was leading.

"Well, a couple of the doctors over in Purcell have been raising a ruckus over him. They say he hasn't been to medical school and that he's killing more folks than he's saving. When you see him the next time, tell him I'm looking for him," Carr said.

"He's been doin' a good job for us," I told him, pointing to the shelf of bullets behind the bar. "He's pulled a fair amount of lead out of some of our best patrons."

"Just the same, I have to find out more about him." He stood straight up and hitched his pants up before sauntering out the door.

Robert came over from the roulette wheel, "What was that all about?"

"Ah, he was askin' questions about Skunkbit and then Linc and his doctorin.' I don't think Linc will appreciate that at all."

"How did your brother get to be a doctor?"

"Well, he started out doctorin' horses and cows and then sort of drifted into people since there weren't many doctors around. As a matter of fact, ol' Skunkbit got him started. After that skunk got him, he went lookin' all over hell's half-acre for a madstone to cure him."

"What is a madstone and what's it supposed to cure?"

"Why, rabies of course. Linc still uses his madstone all the time. One guy came all the way up from Gainesville to get the cure after he was bit by some dog," I told him.

"You still haven't told me what it is," Robert replied, sounding mildly perplexed.

"Linc's madstone is a curved stone about the size of a silver dollar. It's thick in the middle and thinner at the edges. Kind of a dark red stone with streaks of pink. You find madstones in the stomachs and intestines of deer. You put the madstone on the bite and if it sticks, there's poison in the wound. If it falls off, then there ain't no madness. Sometimes it takes two or three days for the madstone to do its work. You have to keep takin' the stone off and boilin' it in sweet milk. If the milk turns green, then you know there's poison bein' drawn out of the stone. Then, you put the stone back on the bite until it finally falls off," I explained.

"You've got to be kidding me," Robert snorted.

"People swear by it," I said. Raising my voice, I hollered, "Hey, Skunkbit. Do you believe those madstones work?"

"You bet. I wouldn't be here today if it weren't for your brother and his madstone. I'm glad he was in the territory at the time. I wouldn't have lasted long at all."

Robert shook his head back and forth to register his disbelief.

"Look, if you ever get bit by a rabid animal, I guarantee you will search high and low for anything whatsoever to keep from gettin' rabies. That is one hell of a way to die. Anyway, Linc cured a few folks with his stone and got paid handsomely for it. He liked that so much, he decided to become a doctor full-time. He's set a few bones, delivered a few babies and carries a bunch of homegrown remedies around with him. I don't use him unless my horse is lame, but you're more than welcome to."

"Thanks, but I think I'll use Doc Goldsby. At least he has a piece of paper on the wall that says he's a real doctor."

"Linc may not appreciate losin' your business," I laughed.

"Can't lose something you never had," he responded, laughing even harder.

"What are you two hyenas cackling about?" Sandy asked with a toss of her head. She'd just come in the back door and was dressed for a busy Saturday night.

Robert whistled. "Don't you look like the winning filly at the Kentucky Derby. You know, you're wasting your talent upstairs."

"How would you know what I'm wasting upstairs?" she threw back at him. "From the sounds of it, I'd be better off running a horse race somewhere. Maybe Tucson."

"If I ever bothered to find out what business is like upstairs, I'd just be giving money to D.W. just to spend time with you."

"Is that so bad? I'd give you some money just to spend time with D.W.," she said in a huff.

I tried to break up the tension a little, "I don't mess around at all. I'm married and Dahlia sure wouldn't take kindly to me messin' around with another woman. As I recall, she said she'd skin me alive with a dull knife."

"Married? You? I don't believe it. Who would want to put up with some reprobate like you?"

I could tell I had broken up their little soiree and had been able to shift their anger - to me. "Now, that's no way to talk about Dahlia. We've been married for eighteen years and have nine kids. She's a good woman. Doesn't give me too much grief and stays home and takes care of the kids."

"Nine kids. What do you do with them? Run guns along with your whiskey? You've got nine kids and run a bar in the middle of a river. I think I have finally heard it all. What am I doing here with two incompetents? I should be in Tucson."

"I think my original comment was that you looked good," Robert interjected. "However, I'm beginning to feel that that's only the case when you keep your mouth shut."

She started looking for a glass or a bottle or something else to throw and I thought it was a wise idea to go check our whiskey supply before I got hurt. Ducking into the back room, I could hear the two of them going at each other. They must really be in love, I thought.

"As soon as I get enough money, I'm leaving this river bottom and I'll never look another dirty cowhand in the face again. I'll find a place as far away from cattle herds as I can get," she said, anger tingeing her voice.

"What the hell set you off?"

"You, you tinhorn gambler. All I'm good for is bringing in some poor dupe that doesn't know the difference between a straight and a flush for you to pick his pocket."

"Now, wait a minute," he said. "I didn't choose your occupation. Nor did I tell you to keep at it. I'm beginning to think D.W. was right. We should have let you go to Tucson."

At that point she let out a low moan and started crying. She ran off towards the stairs and I peeked out through the door. "You silver-tongued devil, you," I said.

"Now what the hell are you talking about?"

"I swear Robert. For a man of the world, you're still learnin' a lot about your local neighborhood."

"For once I would appreciate it if your homespun philosophy could be put in plain words."

"Well, if I was a blind man in a pitch black room, I could see that she was smitten with you."

"Right. This is a business deal. Nothing more."

"That's the way it used to be. Now, she's on the prod and you're her prime target. Don't that just put a light bounce into your dance step," I said.

About that time, the front door slammed open. "Here come the cowboys. Saturday night in Sand Bar Town. "Whoopee," I heard him say as he headed for the tables.

"How long will the civilization of the age endure the present lawlessness of the Indian Territory?" -- Ft. Worth Gazette'
"Until civilization gets enough sense pounded into it to take measures to prevent lawlessness, and also until it offers some inducements besides condemnation for everything that is done in the Territory."

. . . *The Purcell Register, Dec. 3, 1887*

Chapter 8

In the summertime along this stretch of river, there are two things that always seem to hamper business - mosquitoes and ministers. For most of us in the libation business, these two summertime pests just suck the lifeblood right out of us.

The ministers are by far the worst of these pests. They bring their revivals right down to the river so they can baptize the souls they save on the spot. All the while they're railing against our fine establishments as the reason for all the evils ever perpetrated on mankind in the territory. I could have lived a long time without having to listen to their particular brand of converting the heathen. After all, water wasn't made for dunking people under, it was made for smoothing out our fine whiskey.

Unfortunately, Heaven's Gate Saloon was closest to their favorite campsite. Once a revival starts, they spend all day and half the night caterwauling about the evils of John Barleycorn and the temptations of Eve. You'd think those folks would have had something better to do than sit there and listen to that and swat mosquitoes.

The worst of the bunch was old "Foghorn" Ben Fountains. He was always gushing gospel and you could hear him from Noble to Wayne. He wore his long, white hair combed straight back from his forehead, down over his collar. His thick, bushy, white eyebrows jumped up and down every time he bellowed and pounded the podium. He could put the fear of God in the worst Baptist in the territory with one withering stare from those light gray eyes. Foghorn was in his finest form with his voice booming out across the river. He had learned his trade well at that Baptist school down in Waco, Texas. Baylor or some such nonsense, it was called.

His wife, Beverly, was a fine figure of a woman. You could see the bustle on her rear end wagging up and down the aisle of their makeshift church. It was almost worth sitting through one of his sermons just to see her. Almost. You wouldn't believe how often those good Baptist men would ask her to come down the aisle for another church offering.

"Repent ye sinners. Confess your sins here before Almighty God. Be ye reborn in the Kingdom of God. The Lord Jesus has shown the way. Those of you who have faith in God can turn away from the temptations of the flesh and be rewarded in Heaven. The wages of sin is death. Here in the midst of God's glorious works is a monument to evil.

"Sand Bar Town is an abomination in the eyes of God. Like Sodom and Gomorrah before it, Sand Bar Town will feel the wrath of God and all those who succumb to the temptations of the flesh will spend eternity in Hell. When Adam was offered the apple by Eve in the Garden of Eden, the original sin happened. Here in this paradise, you can cleanse yourself of all your sins and be reborn in the spirit. You can dedicate your life to God. Immerse yourself in the healing powers of the waters of life in the name of Jesus Christ. Like John the Baptist in the wilderness, you are among heathens. Whiskey, wanton women, gambling . . ."

At that point in Foghorn's spiel, a shout and cheers went up in Sand Bar Town accentuated by a couple of pistol shots in the air.

". . . are tearing at the roots of decency, are decaying the morals of our youth, are bringing the wrath of God down on your heads."

Foghorn was shaking his finger at Sand Bar Town as he emphasized his last point. His eyes were wide in a cadaverous looking face. The deeply sunken eyes and thin cheeks added to his ominous presence. His hair was falling down around his face. His flair for the dramatic was finely honed after years of practicing from the pulpit. With his right hand, he brushed his hair back away from his face, standing straight. The hand came away from his head, pointing at the congregation.

"You just heard from the heathen. It came from that den of iniquity right there across the river. Heaven's Gate Saloon. Such blasphemy. The brazenness of their perfidy is there for all to see. Be warned," he said, his voice rising and the Bible shaking in his raised right hand. "Anything to do with that place of sinners will not lead you to Heaven. That place is not Heaven's gate, but rather the back door to Hell and all who enter in will surely suffer in eternal damnation."

Skunkbit looked at me and asked, "Does eternal damnation mean that you spend the rest of eternity listening to these preachers?"

"Probably," I replied as I went back inside. "You sure as hell can't shut them up in this lifetime."

"You shouldn't talk about ministers like that," Sandy said. "They're not kidding."

"You can't be serious. Ol' Foghorn don't know no more than you or me or anyone else. He just believes it better than anyone else. I've been listenin' to him for years now. He hasn't changed a single word of that sermon, except for the name of the saloon. He hasn't shut a single bar down in that whole time. If he did that, he'd run out of sinners before his sermon was half over. He needs us to keep the good citizens of the country in his pocket."

"You should have been a preacher," she said. "You like to have your hand in everybody's pocket."

"Not true. I've read the Bible. I don't need no preacher to tell me what's the right way to live. God helps those who help themselves. That's what the Good Book says."

She laughed. "I think it says a little bit more than that."

Gradually, the sound of singing began getting louder. A couple of cowboys came in the door laughing. "You ought to see those Baptists coming down the river. They've got torches and they're singing up a storm."

Everyone in the saloon headed for the door. Sure enough, there was a long parade of revival goers headed for Sand Bar Town. This was the first time that Foghorn had ever ventured to this side of the river. A dozen torches lit the parade that included kids and dogs and people who were wondering what was going on. He stepped up onto a tree that had been swept downstream some time ago.

"The time has come," Foghorn sounded, "to no longer wait for the sinners to come to us. We now have come to the sinners."

I could see a few people disappearing into the dark from some of the other bars. Most of the Indian patrons had come out and were sitting in the sand watching something they knew must be peculiar to white men.

"Why don't you go march down Main Street in Purcell? They've got saloons over there that have sinnin' down to a fine art. They could use a little heavenly guidance," I said to Foghorn. He ignored me.

"Brethren. We are assembled here before these houses of perfidy. Let us pray for these poor misguided souls," he intoned. Bowing his head, he went on, "Lord, give us the wisdom to bring these heathen souls to your loving grace. Give us the strength to smite these houses of ill repute and bring down your wrath on the sinners."

He turned to us, the torches giving his white hair a red halo. It wasn't exactly my image of an avenging angel. His face was barely visible from the light from the saloons. He pointed towards Sand Bar Town and started pacing back and forth.

"I have been here for more than a year and the stench of Sand Bar Town still taints my nostrils. You can no longer ignore the evil that has been brought into this territory."

Someone from the back of the saloon crowd yelled, "We were here first." Our group started laughing.

Old Foghorn didn't miss a beat. "We are here tonight to witness for our Lord. To learn the evils of John Barleycorn and its effects on even the lowliest of people," he said, pointing to me. "This is what happens to you if you continue to flaunt the teachings of the Lord. Your very soul is at risk. Fire and brimstone will be your legacy if you don't save these souls. You will burn in hell and I can assure you there will be no place in heaven for the likes of them."

"I'd a whole lot rather burn in hell with these guys than have to go to heaven to listen to you," I told him. Several folks nodded their heads in agreement.

"The Lord gave us ten commandments. Everyone of those commandments has been broken in Sand Bar Town. Like the quicksand traps the unwary along this riverbottom, so does the evil of Sand Bar Town suck the innocent into oblivion," he thundered, his voice reaching a fever pitch.

One of the drunker cowboys leaned over the porch railing. "Where's this here oblivion? I haven't lived it up in that cowtown yet."

"You mock the messenger of the Lord. You will feel the wrath of God. When it comes time for you to account for your sins, your list will be long and will be your soul's damnation," Foghorn answered. "Is there one among you who can say he is without sin?"

"That makes two of us," Robert chimed in. "Listen preacher, we appreciate your dedication, but it's plumb ruining our Friday night business. Why don't you just go on back across the river and preach to folks that want to hear you?"

I was taken aback. I had never heard Robert use such a tone of voice against anyone. "Look, preacher, we've been listenin' to you for the past few years too. And, we ain't no more moved by your fancy talkin' now than we was then. As a matter of fact, we'd a whole lot rather have your wife preachin' instead of you.

At least we'd have a nice lookin' woman to watch."

For the first time in his life, I do believe, Foghorn didn't have a thing to say. Beverly, however, did. She walked up to me hips swinging in that way of hers, took her hymnal and whacked me across the side of the head. All hell, so to speak, broke out. Foghorn was yelling at Beverly. Beverly was taking another swing at me. Robert grabbed Beverly and tried to pull her off me. Sandy came out on the porch and started cussing at the ruckus. The congregation headed for the melee. The cowboys headed for the congregation. And, the Indians? Well, they just sat there pointing and laughing.

One of the churchgoers had run off across the river and up Depot Hill, yelling his fool head off about the fight at Sand Bar Town and how the preacher and his wife were being assaulted. Deputy Carr was sitting in the Carlton Hotel with a cup of coffee when a couple of people came running up to him. They gave him a somewhat slanted version of what was occurring.

Deputy Carr came riding down Depot Hill with his rifle in a scabbard and shotgun in his hands. He could see the swarm of people wrestling around in front of the Heaven's Gate Saloon. Foghorn's roaring voice could be heard over the din of shouts and curses.

The deputy wheeled his horse up into the middle of the fracas and yelled, "What the hell's going on here?"

He pointed his shotgun up in the air and pulled the trigger. Everyone in the crowd ducked at the sound of the shotgun. "Shut up. Break it up. I'm going to arrest every damn one of you if you don't settle down."

Once the crowd finally got quiet, he looked at the scene. Foghorn was standing there with his hands still locked around Robert's neck. Beverly was standing there with a bloody hymnal and my nose was gushing red blood. Sandy was standing on the porch laughing and pointing. She must have had some Indian blood in her from somewhere.

"All right, preacher, let the man go. Who started this

ruckus?"

Everyone started talking at once, pointing at each other. He fired off the other barrel.

"One at a time. You first, D.W. You look the prettiest."

I stuffed my handkerchief up my nose. "We were here mindin' our own business when Ol' Foghorn brought his flock over here tryin' to fleece us."

"That is an outright lie," Foghorn responded. "We were bringing religion to these sinners."

The deputy raised his hand. "Hold on preacher, I'll get to you in a minute. Keep going, D.W. This whole shebang is starting to wear on me and I haven't been here very long at all."

"Well. He came over here and parked his carcass in front of our saloon and started runnin' off all our customers. We asked him politely to leave and he kept preachin.' I finally told him that I would a whole lot rather watch his wife preach and she hauls off and whacks me with that book."

"Is that right?" he asked her.

She nodded her head up and down.

"All right preacher. Why were you strangling him?" he asked pointing to Robert.

"The man had his hands on my wife. I'll let no one manhandle my wife," Foghorn said.

"Robert?"

"I was just trying to pull her off D.W. She was beating him pretty good with that hymnal. Just look at that bloody mess. I was just trying to break up the fight. She started it."

"Preacher, you and your wife can follow me up to the office. You've still got some explaining to do. The rest of you folks," he said pointing to the congregation, "go on home and stay on your own side of the river. D.W., go fix your nose. Robert, leave the preacher's wife alone. Get those Indians up out of here. They're not supposed to be drinking."

The marshal paused to catch his breath. "You cowboys, this ain't no damned billiard hall. Next time you go to church, sit and listen to the sermon. You haven't got any call to tear the place up. Is that clear?"

There were a few mumbles as the various groups separated and began drifting off home or back into the saloons. The Indians saw that Deputy Carr wasn't in a hurry to leave so they grunted a few times and headed for Purcell. Once they were gone, the deputy walked Foghorn and Beverly back to their tents. After a short time, he left them sitting next to the podium.

I walked back inside and told Robert and Sandy, "Well, the good deputy escorted them back to their tent and left them there."

"It's probably a good thing," Sandy said. "If they ever get you in a courtroom, you'll be the one that goes to jail regardless of who did what to whom."

Robert laughed. "I wonder what it would take to actually get some protection down here along the river. I don't know which is worse, the drunk cowboys and the thieves or those revival preachers."

"It depends on whether you have thick enough skin to stop bullets or a thick enough soul to stop avenging angels," I said.

"The good work of making improvements is steadily advancing here. A brisk trade and competition is making the people realize that it is time to make their property attractive if they would hold custom...."

. . . The Purcell Register, Feb. 25, 1888

Chapter 9

The saloon that seemed to get the most attention was the one with the simplest name - Sand Bar Saloon. Charley and Sam Lissauer built the seedy looking building. The Sand Bar Saloon was Charley's place while Sam ran a saloon on Main Street in Lexington called Little Sam's. He managed to snag all the high-and-mighty drinkers in that fancy place. It was in a brick building with billiard tables to go along with the drinking and gambling.

Someone else built a saloon called the First Chance and Last Chance. There were a few tents and a couple of other buildings that were mainly tin roofs with canvas sides. The only bad thing about tents is that they burn too easily when cowboys start fighting and knock over the kerosene lanterns.

We kept a couple of barrels of water next to the back corners of the saloon just in case we needed to put out a fire quickly. Most of the townspeople would have a whole lot rather come down and put the torch to Sand Bar Town rather than send the fire department to save it.

Although we had a steady business with the liquor and gambling and upstairs, we had to do something to increase the traffic so we could make more money. Robert and I were sitting on the porch one afternoon waiting for the sun to edge down a little further in the sky.

"Have you noticed how much more business Charley Lissauer gets from the Indians than we do?" I asked him.

"Sure do. But, I think I know why."

"It sure can't be the alcohol. They always know when I'm at

71

the still and they line up to refill their jugs."

"Haven't you ever wondered why they have a chant about sundown everyday over there?"

"Can't say I ever really noticed."

"You should have. He's got a painting of Custer's Last Stand on the wall in a special section. Those Indians come in everyday and pray to the painting. Then, they start toasting the victory over and over again. By the time they leave, they're so snockered they can't even see straight. Charley set up that section just for the Indians with a wall that separates them from the rest of the customers. They've got their own door, which is a blanket covering the doorway. Maybe you've seen it? You know, a black blanket with a white buffalo in the middle."

I started chuckling. "That blanket sure do get around. I'm going to have to take Linc over there and show it to him."

"Why?"

"Oh, the last time I saw the blanket it was on George Big Tree. He was sittin' up on Red Hill during the land run. I guess I know where he takes his business now. Anyway, Linc and I have a special place in our hearts for that blanket. We had it before Big Tree got it."

"That sounds like another one of your long-winded tales that I really don't want to hear," Robert replied, quickly changing the subject. "Maybe we ought to put up a few pictures of Indians winning some fights."

"No, that's only one saloon and we have a whole passel of saloons that we have to do something about."

"There's that look in your eye again. I'm not sure I want to hear this one either."

"Now, Robert, was this such a bad idea? You're gettin' to be a rich man. Maybe there's a way to direct more folks to our place."

"All right, I'll bite. What is it this time?"

"What's the one thing that almost everyone complains about when they come in here? At least the ones that walk over here."

"I don't know. Mostly they complain about your cheap whiskey and bad cards."

"No, no, no. Long before they get to the bar or one of the tables, they're complainin' about wet feet."

"So?"

"Let's build a boardwalk from the train depot, across the river and directly to our front door."

"A boardwalk."

"Yep. That way our customers could get here easier and they'd be dry and happy. On the way home, they'd be dry and broke. But, we'd make sure the customers from the trains, especially, saw us first. It wouldn't take much. Put a few pairs of posts across to the far bank. Nail some cross bars and a crosspiece between the posts. Then put some planks down on the crosspieces and there you have it. A whole new way to get customers to the front door."

"What's going to keep the rest of the saloons from doing the same thing?"

"They don't have the business. Charley's place is really the only one that can keep up with us. He's close enough that he won't see any problem with us bringing the train passengers over here more easily," I told him. "It'll be just like the time when we started buildin' the saloon. Only he won't have to build one of these walkways to get some business."

"I think you are absolutely crazy. Damn. I'm beginning to sound like Linc. I know if you come up with a good idea that I'm going to be in trouble," he said, shaking his head. "What's it going to cost?"

"Hell, I don't know. A few posts. A few boards. It can't be too much and every penny will be worth it," I said, daydreaming about the increased number of customers.

"Well, I guess I'd better go into town and get them to work on it," he said. "Nobody in their right mind is going to listen to you. What am I saying? I can't be in my right mind; I'm listening to you."

I smiled and nodded as he went to get his horse. "See," I told him as he headed for the ford, "you don't like to get your feet wet either."

The horse snorted at that moment. Pointing to his mount, he replied, "My sentiments exactly."

With the building of the walkway, the number of rowdies that showed up on our doorstep increased as well. Business began picking up during the day for the drinkers, anyway. I could open up an hour before the next train was scheduled to leave or an hour or two after one arrived and do a booming business. I even hired another bartender to work the morning train shift so I could stay home and get some extra sleep.

The thing about solving one problem is that it always leads to the next problem. The increased foot traffic on the bridge posed a problem that we hadn't expected, but should have. The number of drunks going home at night that couldn't navigate on the narrow planks were giving the frogs and turtles a scare by continually falling in the river. Before the footbridge went in, a lot of them would just curl up behind one of the buildings and sleep it off until morning. At least, the sand was soft.

But now, they thought they could make it with no problem. A lot of the drunks were thrown in the river when sober guys were coming from the Purcell side in a hurry. It wasn't until after the second drunk drowned that our new problem was solved.

I was taking a break out on the back porch, smoking a cigar and breathing in the clear night air when I saw Deputy Carr ride up. He hadn't been through here since the bridge had been put up, so he was eyeing it as he rode up.

"What in the hell are you doing now, D.W.?" he asked.

"If you can't bring the mountain to Mohammed, then bring Mohammed to the mountain, or somethin' like that, I think. We're just improvin' our chances of landin' a few new customers," I said.

"What's this about some fool drowning here the other

night?"

"That was Joe Crockett. You know, Davey's fourth or fifth or was that sixth cousin. He tripped and fell at the exact wrong spot and they fished him out about a quarter mile downstream day before yesterday."

"Was he drinking at your place?"

"Hell, deputy, he was drinkin' at all the places. He'd get rowdy in one and they'd run him out. He'd stumble next door and try another one. He musta been in half a dozen places before he headed home. I didn't see him leave and I shore didn't see him take a nose-dive into the river."

"You know that if this keeps up, I'm going to have to shut this place down."

"You don't have a snowstorm's chance in hell of doin' that. Why are you even botherin' to make a threat?"

"Look here, D.W. There's folks here that are getting downright sick of what goes on down here in the river. They've been sending complaints to the U.S. marshal in Guthrie and he's taking a very dim view of the shenanigans that go on down here. One of these days a whole damn army of marshals are going to come down here and clean this place out."

"I thought you guys were too busy with the Dalton and Doolin gangs to bother with us."

"We've got bigger fish to haul in for sure. If Purcell was in Oklahoma Territory, you guys would already be out of business. They're raising so much hell that somebody's backside is going to get blistered. Since they're in Indian Territory, the folks over here don't pay them as much mind. But civilization is here to stay, and they won't be quiet at all," he said.

"That was quite a speech for you. I don't recall you ever bein' so longwinded."

"Fine. If the footbridge leads to more drownings, it's going to come down."

"It's been taken care of," I told him in my sincerest voice. "As a matter of fact, here he comes now."

"Who?"

"The fisherman, of course."

The deputy looked up to see a Negro about six-feet tall come strolling across the footbridge with a cane pole in one hand and a bucket of worms in the other. He stopped on the bridge over the middle of the river and started baiting his hook. He looked up and waved and I waved back.

"Now, what kind of fool goes fishing in the Canadian this time of year when the water is so hot and shallow?"

"Oh, he just likes to sit and ponder life. He does that by drownin' worms."

"Having someone trying to catch catfish in the middle of summer is not going to help you one bit."

"His name is Jake Summers and he works for a few of us saloon owners."

"You serving fried catfish now."

"No, no. We call him the fisherman because that's what he does. He pulls men out of the river, not catfish. He gets a nickel a head for every drunk he fishes out of the Canadian and if they want to pay him for savin' their hides, he can make some extra money."

"You better hope it works."

"It has so far. He keeps a torch lit in the middle of the bridge and that helps a few of our patrons find their way home. If he does get a mess of catfish, he don't have to spend his money on food."

I watched the good deputy shake his head and ride on towards Lexington. I could tell he didn't think much of our plan, but some plan was better than no plan.

With the footbridge in place, Sandy's business from train passengers started picking up. She now had four girls working for her and kept the rooms upstairs busy all the time. She even put a cot in the storeroom downstairs for men too lazy to climb the stairs.

"Now look, you two goof-offs, I think it's time we started talking about expanding the saloon."

"We don't need anything bigger than what we've got now," Robert said. "This is just the right size for what we need."

It had been some time since I had seen Sandy head upstairs, so I knew she didn't need the space.

"We could always throw a tent up out back," I said. "Be a whole lot cheaper."

"Look, you blockheads," she said in her least pleasant voice. "I'm trying to build up a business that will put this place on the map. If you can't see how much more business we have than other saloons, then you need new glasses."

"So, what do you want?" Robert finally asked.

"Extend this place back another ten or twelve feet and add two more rooms upstairs. Then, I can have a bedroom downstairs in the back," she said.

"What for?" Robert made the mistake of asking.

"What do you think I want it for? I'm going to live right here in the saloon. That way I don't have to worry about getting home safe at night. Besides, I can entertain my very special customers in there."

"Are those the ones that take baths?" he egged her on.

Her eyes narrowed as she bit her lower lip. "I don't know who dropped the coals in your pants, but I don't need to take any crap from you. If you two wonderful businessmen can build a silly footbridge and charge me for it, then by damn we can add on to this building and make that damned bridge worthwhile."

"I can see your point," I put in my two cents worth. "But, do these special customers of yours bring in extra money?"

"I swear," she said in exasperation. Turning to Robert, she waved a fist under his nose. "What in the hell does he put in your drinks? He comes up with harebrained scheme after harebrained scheme and you willingly put your money up for them. I ask for a little help in making a solid business decision and you two jackasses ask about my customers. As long as you get paid, then by damn, my business is none of your business. My special customers won't bring in nearly as much as another two rooms and another girl or two. You both drink too damned much of that rotgut you make."

"Now, we didn't say it wasn't a good idea. We just have to think about it a bit. After all, we did spend a princely sum for that bridge," Robert said, apologizing as fast as he could and looking at me accusingly.

"Now how was I supposed to know that they had to zigzag that bridge across the river so they could find places for the posts to stay put. That made the bridge longer than I had anticipated."

"Now, we have to pay someone to pull drunks out of the river."

"It's a good investment in keeping our customers alive. Otherwise they wouldn't be spending any money at all unless they asked for a wake," I said, defending my position.

Sandy had pulled a derringer from a garter on her right leg. She sent a bullet flying into the crown of my hat, which had been resting peacefully on the hat rack. "I'll make this real simple for the two of you. Either build the extra rooms or I'll hold a wake in your honor after they pull your bullet-riddled bodies out of the river. Do I make myself clear?"

"Very," Robert said, as he put his hat on and headed out the door towards town.

She watched every move he made as he left the saloon, the gun dangling at her side.

"I'll bet you don't have a single special customer to your name," I mused.

That broke her concentration. "What makes you say that?" she murmured as she reloaded the derringer and put it back in its place on the garter.

"Robert doesn't pay nearly as much attention to you as I do. Bartenders are like that, you know. I can see you're taken with him and I think you're tryin' to find a way out of doin' daily chores. As a matter of fact, I think you have quit ridin' the bedsprings."

She sighed, paying little attention to what I had to say. "There are bigger fish in the sea."

"Yeah, but there aren't bigger fish in the river," I added.

"We have frequently heard experts say that the Lexington whiskey was of that quality that three drinks of it would make a man murder his grandmother, and we are inclined to believe it true after listening in the silent hours to the voice of one who had tarried too long on the river's further shore and at midnight reeled past our cottage door yelling in stentorian tones -- 'Hot tamales, on ice!'"
. . . *The Purcell Register, Feb. 20, 1891*

Chapter 10

There is something about a bar that seems to draw flies. Not the six-legged kind, but the two-legged, booze swilling, bar-hugging kind that could hear a bottle being opened a half-mile away and would swarm to a glass of whiskey before the last drop left the bottle.

What makes them even more strange is that they tend to visit the same bar over and over again even though everyone there has heard their stories a hundred times or more. I had three bar stools that sat at the end of the bar farthest from the front door. That end of the bar was almost a shrine to the locals who had seen these three men down enough whiskey to float Old Ironsides. It was long assumed that all three men had cast iron stomachs and that their livers were solid brass.

Theo Spencer was a Confederate veteran who managed to spend most of his monthly income at the Heaven's Gate Saloon. He was a few years older than me and walked with a limp in his left leg. He had a full beard that was streaked with gray and he wore that old kepi well down across his forehead. He had gotten a veteran's allotment in the land run and was leasing it out to a couple of farmers.

Shorty Harbaugh was often called Stumpy because he was so short and round. After a few drinks, though, it didn't make any difference what you called him. He always wore one of those stovepipe hats. He thought it made him taller and taller men got more respect. When it came to putting away the liquor, he had the respect, even awe, of every man in the territory. They figured that he looked like a keg and his low center of gravity let him carry it without tipping over.

Francis O'Donnell was called Irish. He had a brogue that wouldn't quit. His choice of poison was beer. That stuff put a shine on his face that would light up the entire end of the bar. I kept a bat made of bois d'arc under the bar at that end of the saloon for the times when he got his Irish dander up and tried to rearrange that end of our establishment.

"Well, well, if it ain't the three bucketeers. Come here to raise arms and down beer. All for one and one for all, ain't it? You guys think you could get along on one for all?" I asked them one Friday night.

"I do believe that we could get along a lot better with all for one," Irish said. "Besides, the watered down stuff you sell wouldn't wet the whistle of a half-sized gnat."

"Is that why it takes me so long to get drunk?" Shorty asked.

"Hell, no," Theo answered. "Because you're so short, the alcohol goes right through you and doesn't stay long enough to do any damage."

"I see they had a story about your mother-in-law in the paper Irish," I said.

"What the hell are you talking about?" he growled.

"See, here. The June 5th issue. It says, 'A fifty pound turtle, captured on the Washita, has been the center of attraction at Miller & Co.'s Meat Market this week. The varmint can beat an Oklahoma boomer at jumping and snaps worse than an old maid with new store teeth.' Ain't that where your mother-in-law works? How can they tell the difference between the two of them?" I asked.

"Ahh, ye can't make fun of me mother-in-law. She's a pretty decent sort. Besides, she brings us some pretty good cuts of meat from that place at a pretty decent price," Irish laughed half-heartedly.

"Don't worry, Irish. At least, you'll be out of jail. Your two buddies here sound an awful lot like these two guys," I said, pointing to Theo and Shorty. "I think they changed their names. Weren't you both from Arkansas?"

Shorty stood up and you couldn't tell he had left the stool except that he seemed to lose a couple of inches. "You been drinking this turtle pee you call whiskey? What in the hell are you blathering about?"

"I saved this story from the April 10th newspaper. I've been trying to find out if there is a reward for turnin' these two in. You sound just like them."

A groan arose from the three of them.

"All right," Theo said, laughing. "Let's hear it."

"The Register called this one an Oklahoma incident. I bet they followed you down here just to get the details for the story. Pay attention," I said as I read. "'Old Bill Spriggins and old Tom Slumson, formerly of Arkansas, but both citizens of Oklahoma at present, met in an Oklahoma town the other day, when the following conversation and set of events occurred.

"'Hello, Bill, how ar ye?'

"'Well, ding my buttons, howdy Tom.'

"'Fust rate.'

"'So'm I.'

"'Fokes well.'

"'Yaa.'

"'Your'n well?'

"'Yaas.'

"'Git you a place in Oklahoma, Bill?'

"'You bet, did you, Tom?'

"'Yaas.'

"'Is your'n a good place, Tom?'

"'It was at fust, but no count now.'

"'Why?'

"'Caze ther haint a coon on it.'

"'Mine is adzackly the same. I've done kotch every skunk off'n it.'

"'What you livin' on Tom?'

"'Govemint grub. What you livin' on?'

"'Nothin' now. Govermint rations done gin out,'" I continued reading.

Theo started snoring as though he had heard enough.
"Wake that fool up. He's missin' the best part," I told Shorty.

"Read faster," he said.

"All right. This is the part that should get your attention.
It's what made me think of you immediately. It goes on, 'Had
any thing to drink lately?'

"'No.'

"'Would ye like to hev sum now?'

"'You bet.'

"'So'd I.'

"'How're we gwyne to git it?'

"'Got any mon'y?'

"'No; have you?'

"'No; haint had fur some time.'

"'Suthin got to be done, Tom.'

"'Yaas; how'a ye gwine to do hit, Bill?'

"'Doan kno; foller me, ole Bill haint gin up yet'

"They enter a suburban saloon and find the bar tender alone.

"'You jest do nothin' Tom, but whut I tells ye,' whispers Bill.

"'Sartingly.'

"Old Bill approaches the bar, with old Tom following him.
He addresses the bar keeper with, 'Mister, will ye be so kind as
tu giv us sum ov yer best con whiskey this evenin; we's very
cold.'

"The bar-keeper set out two glasses and a bottle of whiskey;
the two men proceeded to drink freely, filling their glasses the
third time, then, after smacking their lips and wiping their
mouths on their coat sleeves, they bid the bar-keeper good day
and started out when the bar-keeper planted himself between
Old Bill and the door in a threatening way and demanded pay
for the liquor they had drank.

"'What's the matter,' demanded Old Bill.

"'I'll show you what,' exclaimed the bar-keeper, seizing him by the collar.

"Suddenly there was a noise like the end of house had fallen in, when the bar-keeper turned up flat on his back on the floor with Old Bill on top of him pounding him lustily.

"'For God sake, old man, hold up; you're killing me.'

"'Yer want pay for the likker ye gin a feller, hey?'

"'No, I don't want any pay and if you will let me up, I'll set em up again.'

"Old Bill lets him up, watching him closely until he again sets out the bottle and glasses, when they both drink freely and walk leisurly out wiping their mouths on their coat sleeves. When they reached the pavement Old Bill turned to old Tom and said:

"'Pears to me some people is orful fools in this kintry, an ye have to mos knock em down before they have any sense.'

"As soon as he could, the bar-keeper ran to find a policeman, but the two friends had disappeared."

"That's the end of the story," I said. "Just sit here till I find a marshal."

"Hell, you've never set a bottle and glasses on this bar without the clink of coins first," Irish said. "But, if you'll just set one up now, I'll have Theo sit on you for the rest of the night. One bottle isn't going to help our thirst at all."

"Why do you even bother reading stuff like that?" Shorty whined. "It just makes the whiskey go down that much harder. Besides, if Old Bill and Tom had tried that around here, they'd have been pulling buckshot out of their hind ends for weeks. You are the unfriendliest bartender I ever met."

"Unfriendly? Look at this warm, fine establishment. Taste that fine whiskey. There's some folks we don't even let in the door. You guys have been sittin' on those three stools so long that the seats are contoured to your butts. Nobody else will sit on 'em because they're so uncomfortable. There's not another bar in the territory that would treat you guys any better," I said.

"It's that cold, blue steel you've got on that 12-gauge shotgun barrel that says unfriendly. It's that cold stare from those dark brown eyes of yours that don't light up till you've got cold, hard cash in hand," Theo replied.

"Besides, you wouldn't call a marshal down here for love nor money," Irish said.

"Well, maybe for money," I chimed in. "You know it's damned hard to hold onto what you make here. You damned near have to have more and bigger shootin' irons than anyone else. The gunfights don't really start till after the saloon closes."

"I don't see no holes in your hide," Shorty mumbled. "Maybe I could get old Bill and Tom to come down and use you for target practice."

"You better have them bring a shovel with them cause old D.W. will be in his hidey hole with the lid pulled down tight," Theo laughed. "A gopher would have an easier time getting at his money."

"Just because you three don't have any money left when you stagger back home doesn't mean it ain't dangerous out here," I answered. "Why just the other day, the guy who owns the River Pearl Saloon lost his little finger when someone took a knife to him. They relieved him of his night's take and gave him his finger back as a warning. Well, I have a saying around here. If somebody want's to do the Heaven's Gate dirty, I'll send him hell."

"See, there," Shorty said. "Some guy trying to make some money and you treat him like that."

"Have another drink, Shorty. You need it," I said.

"Speaking of marshals, how come you never have been run in for making whiskey?" Theo asked. "I swear you've been selling whiskey around here since before the big run. And, I've seen those marshals hauling wagonloads of whiskey peddlers to Ft. Smith and Texas and Kansas."

"That's one of those trade secrets," I said.

"Who you been paying off?" Irish asked, his face beaming with a ruddy red glow.

"All right. It wasn't no payoff. You know Bill Carr. He runs the Fashion Saloon in Lexington, now. When I first came into this part of the country, he was a deputy marshal. He always took a likin' to my liquor. He figured he could afford to turn his back on one bootlegger. He never said anything, but he always managed to let me know when a bunch of unfriendly types were comin' through town. He stills buys a few jugs from me now and then. He likes the taste of it," I explained.

"I'll be damned. Here all this time I thought you was the luckiest duck in this whole damned country," Shorty said. "If I'd known that, I would have turned you in."

"It's too late now, I've already moved my operations to this side of the river. As long as I don't have some ticked off turnkey chasin' me up and down the Canadian, I can make and sell as much as I want," I added.

"Your whiskey does taste different. Why's that?" Theo asked, with a sidelong glance.

"That's somethin' for me to know and you to find out. If I give away all my secrets, then I'll end up with some other fellow puttin' me out of business."

"That don't sound like a bad idea," Shorty said.

"How come you're out here in the middle of the river instead of in Lexington like the best of them?" Theo asked.

"You mean rest of them, don't you?" I said with eyes narrowed.

"Oh, right," Theo snickered.

"I was sittin' up on Red Hill watchin' all the traffic crossin' the river bottom to Lexington and I just knew they'd be happy not to have to walk so far. So, we built it here," I told them.

"That's crazy," the three of them said at the same time.

"I swear. I'm sittin' here makin' money and you're sittin' here drinkin' and all I get are insults," I replied. "I guess I am goin' to have to stop tellin' that story."

"I'll drink to that," Irish said, lifting his glass in a toast.

"Look, you got to do somethin' different to get the business. We get folks off the train that wouldn't go the other half-mile to Lexington. Besides, it's more crowded in Lexington than it is here. Listen to this story. I cut it out of the Jan. 3 paper just to show doubters like you. 'Lexington has more than doubled her population in the past eight months, and can count more saloons in proportion to population than any other town in existence, although, under the new liquor law, some of them will probably close up. A sufficient number, however, will be licensed, to considerably swell the school fund,'" I read. "Out here in the middle of the river, I ain't swellin' no school fund. They're chargin' $2.50 a month for saloons there. Restaurants have to pay $2.00 a month. You'd go broke with a place there."

"Oh, you're full of blarney," Irish said. "You're just too damn cheap to want a fancy saloon. I've been in better buffalo wallows than this."

"You wouldn't know a buffalo if it bit you in the ass," I told him.

About that time, Irish started bellowing "When Irish Eyes Are Smiling." That was the signal for Shorty and Theo to lift him off his stool and carry him back across the river. Another fine night had passed into history.

"TAHLEQUAH, I.T., Feb. 19. -- James Bowen, a prosperous farmer living about three miles south of here, met with a horrible death late yesterday evening by lightning. He was returning from this place with a wagonload of farm implements, and just before reaching home was overtaken by a thunderstorm. As he was passing a neighbor's house a stroke of lightning, probably attracted by the steel plows and other implements in the wagon, killed both himself and the team. So terrible was the electrical stroke that the unfortunate man was thrown several feet out of the wagon and his clothing torn to shreds and set on fire and his shoes torn from his feet. The horses fell dead in their tracks and the wagon was torn to pieces. The work of the lightning was witnessed by the family of the neighbor, Mr. Wallace, whose house stood but a few yards away. Mr. Wallace ran out to extinguish the fragments of clothing on the body and found him black in the face and horribly scratched and mutilated. Bowen was 35 years old and leaves a wife and four children."

. . . The Purcell Register, Feb. 26, 1892

Chapter 11

Into each life, a little rain must fall. Somewhere, someone had told me that little saying as a way of soothing some upset I had in the far distant past. There were farmers all over this territory who would love to have a little bit more rainfall into their lives. A little rain is fine, but a deluge is something else.

In creating Sand Bar Town, one or two minor problems were somewhat overlooked. Well, maybe they weren't exactly minor problems.

The first time a rise in the river came, we lost the footbridge and a few tents. The second time the river came calling was in the middle of one of Foghorn's revivals.

The storm season was late in 1891. Two or three storms had blown through that particular week and the river had been inching upwards since the first squall line appeared. I was standing on the boardwalk wishing I could move the saloon kit and kaboodle up the hill to Lexington.

A granddaddy of a storm was brewing off to the northwest. It was heading down the river valley like a herd of buffalo that stretched from horizon to horizon. The clouds were the darkest purple and black I had ever seen. Lightning streaked through the clouds every other second giving the storm an almost ghostly appearance. The air was so charged with electricity, there was a blue glow around some of the animals hitched to the rails in front of the saloons.

The river valley was quiet. Even the noises from the towns and the saloons were muted as the countryside waited for the storm to break. In the silence, the words from Foghorn's sermon seemed to be coming from a nether world. As always, he was in fine form. His tent was anchored to a tall old cottonwood on that side of the river. He hadn't visited Sand Bar Town again since the marshal had escorted him away.

The torches were shining brightly in the gloom caused by the approaching storm. Even from where I was standing, I could see how nervous the people and the animals were. Every lightning flash and roll of thunder made everyone in the tent jump. A few of the folks closest to the rear entrance began sneaking out the tent flap.

Traffic between Purcell and Lexington increased quickly as people hurried home before the storm broke.

Robert stuck his head out the front door, "What's going on?"

"We'd better get our backdoor rescue system in place. The river is startin' to rise and that storm looks like it's dropped a bunch of rain upstream."

"Damn. There goes another Friday night and probably Saturday, too."

"Better that than floating down to Arkansas," I replied, heading out the back door towards the wagon we kept in case of a rise in the river. We rousted Sandy out of her quarters and started packing.

"That's it," she said, stringing a few curse words after that statement. "I'm not coming back here. I can't live like this. I've ruined three pairs of shoes walking through water to Lexington.

I'm taking out a place in town and you two can go to hell."

Another lightning flash and roll of thunder added emphasis to her words. The wind had picked up and eddies began whipping sand around the buildings.

"This is the third or fourth time the river has come up. We lose money every time," she ranted on. "I don't know how you think you can keep this up."

"Now, Sandy," Robert said. "At least we haven't lost much. Those guys in the tents lost everything. A lot of them have moved on and we still have a steady bunch of clients. We'll be back in business in a couple of days. Don't worry."

"I can't keep my best girls' backsides pressed against a mattress long enough now to make any money. They'll take one look at that river and stop at the railway station to pick up a john or two. As a matter of fact, that's what I think I'll do," she said, a malicious smile spreading across her face. "That way I won't have to share any income with you two yahoos. Those Oklahoma Territory farmboys are a real pain in the ass. What I need is a lonely banker."

With that she flounced out the back with Robert in hot pursuit, in more ways than one. I went back to the front of the saloon and checked on Skunkbit and a couple of his friends. I headed out the front door and damn near had the door jerked out of my hand by the wind. As soon as I stepped out on the porch, I knew I had made a mistake. The breeze brought Foghorn's voice across the river so very loudly and so painfully clearly.

That didn't worry me nearly as much as the river. By this time, the water was up another foot and I hadn't been gone that long. I could tell by the sound of the storm and its fierceness that this would be a real frog strangler. The only one left listening to Foghorn was his wife. She was trying to get him into their wagon, but he would have none of her cajolings. I knew he could see the river was rising from the reflections from the lanterns in the saloons. He just knew that he was calling down

God's wrath on Sand Bar Town.

"Mighty is God's hand. Terrible is His sword of justice. Here in the depth of this storm, He brings down the Sodom and Gomorrah of Oklahoma Territory. He has brought me to Jordan's soothing waters to witness His retribution," he bellowed.

"Ben, get down off that platform," Beverly said. "You should have enough sense to come in out of the rain."

He turned to her in an exaggerated bow and pointed across the river to Sand Bar Town. Even though he could have talked to her in a normal voice, he was caught up in the excitement of the moment. "Can you not see what is happening here? All these years I have waited for the moment when I could watch the destruction of this den of iniquity. Here it is, woman. Can you not see this glorious moment before you?"

"Ben, there's a storm almost on top of us. You can watch the town being swept away from the safety of the wagon."

"No, Beverly. Here is the answer to my fervent prayers. I am calling down God's wrath here and now. I will be here to direct the storm and avenge all the sins and transgressions that have gone on here."

"You know that is blasphemous. You did not call up this storm and you cannot direct it. What do I need to say to you that will bring you inside?"

"Nothing. I am going to stand here and watch the waters sweep clean the sand. There is nothing for you to say."

"Oh, Ben," Beverly said.

I could see that she was crying by the way she held her hand-kerchief to her face. Old Foghorn came down to the riverbank just above the swirling, black waters. The lightning and thunder were almost continuous. I watched several bolts of lightning light up where Foghorn was standing as bright as day. The wind was whipping his hair around his face and the first large drops of rain began to fall.

The river was rising much faster now and I could hear the

splash of the water as it rose over the boardwalk. I looked out back and made sure that Robert and Sandy had taken the wagon up the hill to Lexington. I walked back through the saloon and picked up a few other things, like the cashbox, and chased Skunkbit out the back door. As I went outside to where my horse was tied to the back porch, I could see that he had lifted an extra bottle for his long journey to shore. I let him go since he was such a good customer. The wind was coming strong out of the northwest, so I mounted and moved the horse around to the south side of the saloon and sat out of the wind to watch the river and Old Foghorn.

My horse started dancing around and I wondered what was the matter. I talked to him a little bit and then looked down at where the ground was supposed to be. The horse was now standing in about six inches of water. As soon as I realized how fast the river was rising, I saw one of the tents floating by in the lamplight. At that same moment, I heard a hideous sound. It took me a few moments to realize that I was listening to Foghorn cackling at the plight of our town. I didn't have time to ponder that, though, and I turned my horse around and headed for higher ground. By the time I reached the foot of the main street in Lexington, the rain was coming down hard. I rode into the shelter of a barn and dismounted out of the wind and rain.

Looking back across the river, I could see Foghorn in the occasional flashes of lightning still standing there, bareheaded, in the rain. A huge bolt of lightning lit up the whole riverbed, striking a tree over by the depot. In that flash, I could see two or three of the wooden saloons start to skew around. There was some water moving in that river this night. Foghorn had seen the same thing, I knew. Although I couldn't hear him, I could imagine him over there taking full credit for the disaster that had befallen Sand Bar Town. Of course, Foghorn wouldn't see it as a disaster at all.

He had chosen a small knoll at the foot of Red Hill to set up his tent this time. It was further away from Sand Bar Town but closer to his flock. To get to the edge of the river, he had to walk over the railroad tracks and come a distance of about one hundred feet. The water had to be six feet or deeper in the main channel by now. It was rising fast enough to force Foghorn back up the embankment toward the railroad tracks. After he watched the last lantern disappear in the dark waters, he walked back up to the knoll. He was about 75 feet in front of his revival tent at the highest point of the knoll. He was silhouetted by the light from the tent opening. Turning to face the river, he stretched his hands skyward, beseeching or thanking or something-ing to the Lord.

At the moment of his triumph, he stood ramrod straight in the dark night. Without a doubt, he cut the finest figure of a Bible-thumper I had ever seen. And then, a blinding flash of light, followed in less than a second by the most Godawful sound I had ever heard, froze me in my tracks. I couldn't see a damn thing and my ears were ringing as though the northbound train was passing through my skull with its whistle going full blast. My horse was shaking so bad that I thought it would unsaddle itself.

There was a brief lull in the storm following that lightning bolt as if that light and sound had been the be all and end all of thunder and lightning. I heard a strange wailing, but it wasn't the wind. My eyesight had returned somewhat and I followed the sound of the wailing across the river. The noise seemed to be coming from in front of Foghorn's tent. The lightning and thunder returned with the rush and one brilliant flash showed me a woman bent over something on the ground.

My mind was still a little befuddled by the thunder so it took a few moments before I realized that bolt of lightning must have struck down Foghorn right in front of his church. The rain returned with a roar and the river was out of sight by then. I waited for the rain to let up a little and walked my horse up the street to a livery.

I walked into Sam's Saloon and saw the two Lissauer brothers sitting at the bar. I took off my slicker and hung in on a rack by the door. "How's business tonight, boys?"

"You damn well ought to know. This ain't a fit night for man nor beast," Charlie said.

"You ain't goin' to like what happened in the middle of the river, then," I told them. "The water's up seven or eight feet deep and all the buildings I could see through the storm were headed downriver."

Sam looked at Charlie. "I told you it wouldn't last out there," he said.

"Now, Sam, this is just a minor setback. We can get back up and running shortly," Charlie pleaded with him.

"I'm a businessman, not a riverboat gambler," Sam replied. "You can open up a place here in town or work with me. I'm not throwing any more money into that river."

"What are you going to do, D.W.?" Sam asked.

"Don't have much choice, I'm afraid. We don't have a fancy place like this to fall back on. There's still some money to be made out there."

"You could still supply us some of your whiskey. I'll pay you good money for it."

"Naw. It's the only thing some of my customers keep coming back for," I laughed. "Or maybe it's the womenfolk we keep around the place."

Sam squinted a bit at that and Charlie looked kind of glum.

"A funny thing happened down on the river in the middle of all this," I said. "I swear Old Foghorn got his comeuppance in that storm. Did you hear that thunder a while ago?"

"Damn right, we did," Charlie said. "Every glass in the house tinkled from that sound. The windows looked like they were going to fly apart."

"If he was struck by lightning, there must be some kind of story in that," Sam said.

"Yeah," I replied. "He's been after Sand Bar Town for years. Looks, like he waited around just long enough to see it off."

"Where was he?"

"Standin' on that knoll just outside his tent."

"In this storm?"

"You bet. I could hear him before the rains came and his wife couldn't get him to come in out of the storm," I said. "You know, sometimes in this world, it's real hard to tell the sinners from the saints."

"A Lexington, Oklahoma, schemer is building a boat to plow the shifting sands of the South Canadian. The remarkable feature about the boat is that it will be used as a saloon, and the thirsty pilgrim from the prohibition land of the Chickasaws can take his 'straight' or 'mixed' at the very water's edge. This is a great age we're living in. - Chickasaw Chieftain."

... The Purcell Register, Nov. 8, 1890

Chapter 12

One thing about a good flood is that all the trash that was outside the saloons gets washed away. In the case of Sand Bar Town this time, though, all the saloons went along for the ride too. A couple of the saloon owners found their tents a few miles downstream snagged in the top of a couple of willow trees. The only thing left of the Heaven's Gate Saloon was a memory.

This time around, the Lissauer brothers decided to keep their feet on dry ground in Sam's Saloon. They weren't ready to put any more money into something that was gone with the water so often. They sold the Sand Bar Saloon to Tom Farmer. Now Tom was a bit smarter than most saloon keeps. He could see that the only way to keep the saloon open for very long was to turn it into a boat - or at least a flatbotomed barge. When the river came up, he only had one problem. The Ark, as it was called, would usually end up partially sunk in quicksand a few miles down the river. The bow of the boat would be pointing upwards at a 45-degree angle and the back third of it would be buried in the sand. At least he could salvage something.

I must admit that building a boat and putting a saloon on it made a lot more sense than watching the river chew up a regular saloon. It took a little longer to convince Robert to go back into business, but he knew it would be worth it.

"I tell you what, D.W., this will be the last time. If this doesn't work, I'm moving on," he told me. "I've got a good grubstake and I don't want to spend it on sending lumber to New

96

Orleans."

"Don't waste another minute sweatin' over the anvil," I said. "I found an old riverboat captain who can build us a good boat. We can run a couple of thick ropes over to the east bank there and keep it from floatin' too far downstream when the river comes up."

Sandy came tromping down the bank to the sand bar. I could see her dander was up and she was a fight waiting to happen. I put Robert between myself and her, just to be on the safe side.

"Now, I've seen everything," she said, smiling, "two ostriches in the middle of Oklahoma Territory with their heads out of the sand for a change."

"Who is this person?" I asked, looking at Robert.

"Oh, shut up, you old fool," she said, her familiar expression of disgust on her face. "This is just a beautiful day. I have been waiting for more than a year to tell you that I told you so. Look at this, all our money and hard work, gone in the blink of an eye. But, that's all right. I got the train schedule for Dallas and then to California. I'm ready for a change of scenery and this is as good a time as any."

"Don't rush off yet," I drawled. "We're buildin' us a boat saloon."

"Any boat you build wouldn't float," she snorted. "It'd have as many holes in it as you do in your head."

"Now, now, pretty little lady, don't you worry your pretty little head about the new business. I'm sure that some conductor on one of those trains will drop you off somewhere in West Texas where nobody will hear of you again and I won't have to listen to you," I replied.

She went up to Robert and cooed in a sweet voice, "Darling, let me borrow your gun. I need to take care of a deranged madman that's blabbering in the middle of this riverbed."

Sandy almost got the gun out before Robert caught her hand. He held her hand and put the gun back in his holster. For some reason, he had a worried look on his face.

"He's right, Sandy. I think we ought to rebuild the Heaven's Gate and fix it so we don't lose it again," he told her.

A whole string of emotions played across her face from surprise to consternation to sadness to downright anger. "Why you dirty, rotten, sidewinding snake of a man. We've been planning to move out of here for months. You aren't backing out on me now."

My left eyebrow shot upward. "What do you mean plannin' to move on? I ain't heard anythin' about that. What's she blatherin' about?"

Robert was set back on his heels. He was trying to get out of that situation faster than a sidewinder rattlesnake in a dust storm. He looked from one of us to the other. "Give me a moment and I'll explain all this."

"Robert," I said, "let me borrow your gun. I finally figured out what madman she was talkin' about."

Sandy was standing there with her arms straight down at her sides and her fists balled tight. She was obviously more of a threat to him than I was, so he talked to her first.

"Look, honey, this is a great chance to put together a really big hit. We don't have a bit of competition out here and the Lissauers aren't going to rebuild the Sand Bar Saloon. We could make a bundle of money this summer with them opening a couple of new areas to homesteaders. There's still some money to be made. We didn't lose nearly as much as the rest of these. You can hold on for one more shot at this saloon."

"Don't honey me, you maggot-infested sack of horse manure. I don't want to work in no damned river no damned more," she said, crossing her arms waiting.

"All right. All right. What can I do to convince you to stay for a few months more?" he begged. It was the first time I had seen this fine figure of a man reduced to such a pathetic sight. I knew I probably should have shot him and put him out of his misery right then. But, I didn't have my shotgun with me.

"You're serious," she said, staring up at him, with a calculating look in her eye that I wasn't sure I cared for at all. She looked at him, then her feet, him again, her feet again, then finally, him, "You're going to have to build the upstairs just the way I want it. I don't want any guff from your silly partner there. Four big rooms and a fancy staircase at the front of the saloon. None of this climbing up the back stairs any more. Four poster beds. Down mattresses. Dressers with fancy mirrors. Bathtubs and water to wash these filthy cowboys.

"And, I don't want to pay for a damn bit of it," she said with a smug look on her face.

Robert turned his woebegone face to me looking for some sympathy. "How about it, D.W.?"

"Wait just a minute here, darling. Am I to understand that you want me to help pay for all her gewgaws so you and her can run off whenever she gets the right grip around your balls?"

"D.W., I've gone along with everything you asked for. It wouldn't hurt you to help me right now."

Boy, did he sound pitiful. "I tell you what. You put up seventy-five percent of the new place and I'll put up the rest. That way she'll know that you have a financial interest in makin' her happy," I said.

He bent his head down and rubbed his eyes with index finger and thumb of his left hand. You could almost hear the conversation that was going on between his ears but he managed not to say what he was thinking. He looked at Sandy one more time.

"It's a deal. Get your riverboat captain down here and tell him what we want. Tell him we'll need it within the next two weeks."

"Sure thing, partner. You just take good care of that pretty little lady and I'll make sure the boat floats."

With that, Sandy stomped off towards town and Robert took his hang-dog expression along behind her.

I waded across the river and walked up Depot Hill to the

Compton Hotel to find Captain Josiah Rollins, otherwise known as Pegleg Pete. He was a short man, with a beard that ran across his chin. If he had been born with red hair, he could have passed himself off as a leprechaun. His left leg from the knee down was made of solid oak. I had seen him nearly beat a guy to death with that leg after the poor fellow insulted Mark Twain.

"Hey, Captain," I said, walking up to him on the front porch of the hotel, "you've got a two-story boat to build."

"That's funny. I don't recall anything about two stories. All I was going to build was a flat-bottomed boat for ferrying folks across that little stream down there," he answered.

"Well, it's got to float, but it needs to be big enough to hold a saloon and parlor. We need room for tables and a bar on the lowest deck and four bedrooms on the upper deck. Needs a good roof, too," I explained. "You know, make it look like the back end of a sternwheeler without the paddlewheel. I want it so it doesn't have to float very far. Tie a rope off so we can pull it to shore when a flood comes through."

"Aye, ye are a bit daft as my Irish friend would say. You don't have the right kind of wood and you don't have the right kind of anything to build a boat."

"Tell me what we need and we'll get it."

"Don't mess with me, laddie. The only ship I want to navigate is my fishing boat on some lake somewheres. You need to have your head examined. You're crazy to want a boat built around here. There's no navigable water and not very much good water for mixing with my whiskey," he laughed.

"Look, we'll pay you a handsome sum to build us a saloon on a boat or a barge or a damn big raft. It can sit on the sand until the river rises. Then, it needs to float."

He eyed me kind of strangely. "You really want a boat, don't you?"

"You bet. Build me a good one and you can have a free drink at my place every day for the next year."

He squinted, his leathery face showing the strain of thinking. "Make it two drinks and you've got a deal."

I stretched out my hand and we shook. "You can get started tomorrow. I need to have something built pretty damn quick. The faster you get it built, the sooner you can belly up to the bar."

"Whose idea was it, anyway, to build all those saloons in the middle of the river?"

Once again, I had that feeling that I knew where this conversation was headed. "Mine."

"What kind of a damn fool would build a saloon in the middle of a river? Now, I know you're crazy."

"That's why we need a boat. So not everybody will think I'm so crazy."

"Fair enough. Come back tomorrow morning and I'll give you a list of what I need. The boat ain't gonna be fancy. I'll just call it a houseboat. You can turn the house into a saloon if you want to. This'll make history, you know."

"All I want it to do is make money," I said.

Within the next two weeks, Pegleg Pete whipped up a really ugly flatbottomed boat that had sides about three feet high. He floated it in the river to make sure the tar in the joints would hold. It took four teams of mules and a couple of brace of oxen to drag that damn thing up on the sand. By then, the Sand Bar Saloon was up and running and a bunch of tents were back in business.

Another week and the shell of the two-story building rose above the boat's deck. Within the next week, the saloon and gambling hall started up again, which couldn't have come at a better time considering how much money we were spending on this project. When we moved the furniture in, we had to listen to all the catcalls from the drunks at the other place. Then, we added a sign that said anyone who went upstairs would have to take a bath and that it was all a part of the service. After, the third bullet hole in the sign, we decided not to push that part of the business too hard.

We even bought a bottle of champagne to christen the new boat. But, we couldn't waste such an expensive bit of booze. So, we broke a jug of my finest over one corner of the boat. We had to build a set of stairs so people could get over the railing without too much trouble.

Finding a place to anchor the saloon was a much bigger problem than I thought it would be. You can't stretch a rope over a mile from shore and not expect it to rot. We figured that having a couple of teams of mules standing by just in case would be the only way to move it quickly. We found the biggest tree in Lexington nearest the river and attached a couple of hundred feet of chain. Then we could pull the saloon over and attach the chain.

Sandy was a whole lot happier with her new arrangements. Business was booming with the new saloon. She now had the finest stable of fillies north of Fort Worth, west of Ft. Smith and south of Dodge City. And, all the stallions in the territory came to sample the herd. By this time, Robert and Sandy were acting as though they actually were married, so she spent all her time downstairs. I wasn't sure how this was going to affect the payment system, but the coins were ringing in the cash drawer and that's all that mattered.

"Ahoy, Cap'n," Irish shouted as he came through the door. "Tis a stormy sea we're havin' to cross tonight. Batten down the hatches and open up the bottles. We'll be toastin' old Ireland tonight."

"What's the occasion?" I was foolish enough to ask.

"Tis the anniversary of when I left Ireland when I was a boy."

"I thought you celebrated that three or four months ago?"

"It took a long time to get off the boat," he bellowed, laughing uproariously.

"Now, this is the kind of ship we should have had comin' over from Ireland," he said. "It wouldn't float very far, but by the time you got there you wouldn't care anyway."

"Now, Irish, Cap'n Rollins assured me that this here boat

was shipshape and would float all the way to the Gulf of Mexico. Of course, I haven't seen him since I paid him off so I'm not sure how much trust he put in his own construction."

Shorty was practically dragging Theo through the door. They were arguing mightily and Theo had the look of a one-legged man in an ass-kicking contest.

"That's a bunch of blarney and you know it," Shorty said.

"I tell you it's bad luck. Next thing you know, they'll have black cats coming out of the back room," Theo replied.

"Tell this overblown fool that this ain't really a ship and that having women on board is not bad luck," Shorty pleaded.

"Why, Theo, this ain't really a ship and havin' women on board is the best thing that could have happened to us," I said. "What brought all this on?"

"Oh, this old fool thinks we're getting ready for an ocean voyage. I told him the only part of this place that would make it to the ocean would be the splinters left after it smashed up along the river."

I nodded my head in agreement. "That is probably closer to the truth than I care to admit. Whether we have women on board or not really won't make a difference. Hell, Theo, have a drink. It'll go away. I promise. Here I'll give you some of my finest, smoothest rotgut."

Irish's head swiveled up. "Did I hear 'give us some?'"

"Just for tonight, the first shot is half-price," I said.

"Ye're just like me tight-fisted old mother-in-law. As a matter of fact, ye're uglier than she is," he sneered.

"Okay. For you, I'll double the price on the drink, then you'll feel right at home," I said, winking at him.

"You know what they're starting to call this thing?" Shorty asked.

I shrugged, not really caring what they called it.

"The Ark. It looks like Noah's Ark, what with the bow and the railings and the house on it. The first time they see cows and horses and sheep lined up to come on board, they're going to be in line," he laughed.

"Now that's a hell of a way to get a reputation," I replied. "After we rebuilt our gaming establishment, though, Robert wouldn't let me keep my Heaven's Gate name. He said we had to come up with a name that described it better."

"Ye finally named it the Wild Irish Rose," Irish piped up.

"Not hardly," I said as I polished a board I was keeping behind the bar. I took it out and hung it over the mirror. "Boys, welcome to the Floating Palace Saloon."

"We are told that much Purcell money is being left in Lexington these nights. The seductive click of the ivories is the entrancing sound that woos the wealth from the pockets of some sports. Games of all kinds from faro to craps, run nightly and ample opportunity is afforded to those who wish to try their luck across the green table."
. . . The Purcell Register, Aug. 14, 1891

Chapter 13

    Towards the end of summer when all the crops were being brought in and the cattle were rounded up for shipment north and south, a lot of money was moving through Purcell. The cotton buyers came into town along with the livestock shippers and all the other well-heeled types looking to buy low so they could sell high elsewhere.

    Robert had been able to tone Sandy down just a bit and dressed her in some fine threads. She looked every inch a lady, as long as she kept her mouth shut. Every morning, he spent in the lobbies of the hotels in Purcell trying to set up a high-stakes poker game every evening.

    The Dalton gang was running around robbing trains and lifting money off passengers, but Purcell wasn't hit too often. By now, Purcell was a big enough town to need two U.S. deputy marshals. The railroad kept guards on duty around the depot because of the switching yard. The city had a couple of constables. And, since the railroads ran straight through this part of the territory, a steady stream of deputy marshals stepped off the train here.

    Most of the goings-on in Sand Bar Town didn't get reported to any of the marshals. The less attention we got the better. Because it was easy to fade away into the willows and cotton-wood trees, a lot of the outlaws spent time in our riverside resting places. Most of them didn't bother us, but a few of them tried. If a large enough gang stopped in, we'd have to give in rather than fight them.

That's when our hidey holes came into play. We kept most of our money in the back half of a keg. The front half always had beer in it while I'd drop the money in the back. I don't know where Sandy kept hers, but I never saw her get robbed. I figured that anybody crazy enough to try to take a nickel off her would have that hellcat after them until they were warming themselves by the fire in hell, which would probably end up being a far better place to stay.

In late September 1891, Robert finally got some sheep to shear. One was a salesman for a line of farm implements. He wore a plaid suit and a bowler hat. He considered himself a real dandy and by the time Sandy was done setting him up, he was a fat turkey waiting to be plucked.

A couple of big shots from the railroad decided to visit the gaming table too. The fifth hand was being played by a cattle buyer from Wichita who was going to make a name for himself in the territory. Unfortunately for him, he wasn't going to like the reputation he would earn.

That Friday night started off somewhat normally. Robert's game was just getting interesting when three men came in dressed in light, brown dusters with their hats pulled low over their faces. Each man looked like a walking Army post with everything but the eight-pound cannons. They strolled up to the bar, their eyes darting everywhere. Once they reached the bar, two of them leaned across towards me while the other one watched the front door. One of them pushed his hat back and I recognized him immediately.

"Well, well, if it ain't the howler from Bitter Creek himself," I welcomed him. "You've been here two minutes and I ain't heard you howl yet."

Newcomb laughed. "Do I know you? You seem awfully friendly for a barkeep in this hell hole."

"Why yes," I answered. "You and Tulsa Jack and a guy named Charlie. And, oh yeah, the crazy one, Black-Faced Charley Y'all sat down with me for a game of poker a year or so ago, but the other guy that was playin' with us fell over in a dead faint."

The one facing the door looked back over his shoulder. "That's right. You're the one that took all my money," Blake said, eyeing me up and down.

The other one leaning over the bar pushed his hat back. "I'm the not-so-crazy Charlie," Pierce said. "You got a pretty good memory. Why don't you pour us some of that rotgut of yours?"

I set out three glasses on the bar. "What are you three boys doin' back this way?"

"We're just scouting around. You know, the fewer questions you ask, the healthier you could remain," Bitter Creek said.

"Now that you mention it, I did read something about Black-Faced Charley the other day. He got his wish from what it sounded like," I said, swiftly sashaying out of a predicament.

"Yeah," Pierce said. "Him and his hell-firing minute. He was shooting that deputy marshal at the same time the marshal was shooting him. They both emptied their guns and I heard that they didn't miss a single time."

"I hated to see Black-Faced Charley go down like that," Tulsa Jack said. "Of course I hate to see any of my pards go out like that."

I poured a second round and added a glass for myself. "Well, this round is on the house. Here's a toast to Black-Faced Charley Bryant. He went out in a blaze of glory just like he wanted to. Not many men can boast of that."

"What can we do for you gentlemen this evenin'?" I asked.

Tulsa Jack pointed to Robert's table. "That looks like a pretty good game. I think Bitter Creek and I would like to join them. You could watch the door, Charlie."

"Hey, wait a minute. I'm a better player than Newcomb ever thought about being," Pierce said.

Tulsa Jack snickered, "Hell, I know that. I want to win some money, not give it to you."

All three men laughed. The two men walked over to the table and looked at the group. They took their dusters off and put them on the table next to the game. "Deal us in."

Robert started to protest, but I waved him over before he could say a word.

"Look, ol' hoss, why don't you just let them sit in with you," I whispered to him. "You don't want to mess with these fellows."

"What the hell are you talking about," Robert hissed. "I've been trying to set up a big game like this for months. These guys look like they're as poor as church mice."

"Yeah, but they got a lot of guns and a whole potful of bullets. The guy with the dark mustache is Tulsa Jack Blake. The sandy-haired one is Bitter Creek Newcomb. They're part of the Dalton gang."

He straightened up when he heard that. He reached over and grabbed me by my lapels and pulled me off my feet. "What?"

"They're okay. They pay for their fun," I told him. "I think."

"Hey," yelled Tulsa Jack, "are you two dancing or are you going to play some cards?"

I glanced at Robert and gave him a somewhat encouraging smile. "Just play your best game and I'm sure they'll go along with it."

Robert let go of my lapels and I dropped back down on my feet. He walked back to the table and sat down opposite Tulsa Jack. Both of the outlaws sat facing the front door with their backs to the walls. Pierce walked over to the table where Sandy was sitting and struck up a conversation with her. He sat where he could watch both the front and back doors.

"Five-card stud is the game, let's see the color of your money," Robert said. Both outlaws took a hundred dollars out of their wallets and laid it on the table. Robert already had a tidy sum in front of him and the other players had been winning and losing money to each other. It looked as though someone had thrown a wet blanket on a hot fire. You could almost see the smoke coming from their ears.

"This place used to be something else," Tulsa Jack stated. "Hell's Half Acre or the Garden of Eden or some such religious nonsense."

"Heaven's Gate," Robert replied.

"You call this the Floating Palace. What is it floating on? A patch of quicksand," Tulsa Jack said, laughing as he won his first hand with three eights.

"No, our first place got washed down the river, so we built this just like a flat-bottomed boat. That way, when the next flood comes, we can float it to shore and move it out on the sand again when the waters go back down," Robert explained.

"That's probably a pretty damn good idea," Tulsa Jack went on. "You must have thought of it."

"No, actually, D.W. did," Robert said, pointing to me. I smiled and waved.

"That old sot. If'n he came up with this idea, I think I'd throw me a canoe out back. Just in case," Tulsa Jack added.

"It wouldn't be the first time he was called crazy," Robert said.

"An' it won't be the last," Irish roared.

"You making much money at this place?" Bitter Creek asked.

"Not right at the moment," Robert told him. "We had to put all our money into building this new saloon. We're still paying for all this furniture."

I always admired how smooth Robert was when he was lying through his teeth. I brought the whole table a round of drinks and charged it off to Robert's bill just to keep him honest, sort of. I was wondering how long it would be before it dawned on the railroad men that these were the bandits that had been holding up their trains and most likely the money they were using was from the express safe on one of their lines.

"What brings you boys out so heavily armed?" one of the

railroad men finally asked.

Bitter Creek looked at Tulsa Jack and winked. "We've been riding guard for a couple of cattle ranchers up in the Strip. Our bosses sold some cattle down in Fort Worth and we were keeping them safe. You know how bad the railroads are about protecting their passengers."

The short, bald railroad man cleared his throat. "I beg your pardon. Our railroad has one of the finest records for delivering goods and money without interference from the riffraff in this territory."

"How do you do that?" Bitter Creek asked. "Send it through Illinois and Tennessee and back through Mississippi and Louisiana?"

"Nah," Tulsa Jack laughed. "They send it through the territory on the stage coaches. It's safer that way. Nobody would be waiting for a railroad shipment on the stage."

"You don't seem to have much faith in the railroad," the taller man said.

"No. I've seen what can happen when five or six men want to rob a train. If you don't have some firepower and a few men with a little sand, those train robbers will take you for every cent you've got," Bitter Creek went on. "Why I heard the Daltons made a haul up near Wharton. Took that train for twenty thousand dollars. And robbed every single passenger, except for the women."

"That's a bald-faced lie," the short man snapped. "You shouldn't be spreading stories like that. Those men didn't get more than a thousand dollars in that holdup and the marshals are on their trail. They'll be in custody in a matter of days."

"Hey, barkeep," Tulsa Jack yelled. "Better not bring another round. These two gamblers have been drinking too much already."

"You don't know what can happen to a group of ruffians like that when the financial power of the railroad is brought to bear on such a problem," the tall one explained.

"Yeah, but you don't know the Daltons. I used to work with Emmett Dalton up on the Turkey Track. He used to tell me stories about Bob Dalton picking gnats off a horse's butt at a hundred yards with that rifle of his. It don't make any difference how much financial power you think you have. In this part of the country, the railroads and the banks have been running over people for years. Sucking the lifeblood out of them and calling it progress. Don't nobody around here care one way or the other what the railroad thinks. Hell, the folks around here are always telling the Daltons what you railroad guys are doing," Bitter Creek said.

"That's the damndest speech I ever heard from you," Tulsa Jack chided him. "You running for territorial governor or something?"

"Deal, you donkey's rump," Bitter Creek said, "or I'll shoot you and turn you in for a reward. You look just like one of those guys from the James gang. You're related to them Youngers, right?"

"Those guys are rotting in prison somewhere," Tulsa Jack said. "Speaking of rotten, that's just what that little speech of yours was. Sorry I ever said a thing about it."

"Set up another round," Bitter Creek said, pushing a ten-dollar gold piece over to me. "Just keep bringing them till the money runs out."

The outlaw reached over and took a drink before raising his glass. "A toast to our railroaders here," Bitter Creek went on. "May you meet the Dalton gang on your next train ride and may you find out that what I've been telling you is God's honest truth."

Everyone but the two railroad men drank to the toast. Tulsa Jack and Bitter Creek seemed to be having a good time bearding the old goats. The game was going pretty much in a two-way split between Tulsa Jack and Robert. I was real glad that I didn't have to play Tulsa Jack very long in that previous game. He was a damn good poker player for a cowboy.

Along about midnight, the railroad men and the peddler were tapped out. The cattle buyer was down a little, but not enough to be hurting. Tulsa Jack had taken most of Bitter Creek's money and was enjoying himself mightily. As the game broke up, Tulsa Jack and Bitter Creek went over to the table with Charlie Pierce. Sandy had long ago given up trying to get any money out of Pierce for any of her girls' services.

As the railroad men started through the door, we could hear a commotion outside. The two men backed into the saloon with their hands held high. I ducked behind the bar for my shotgun and Robert joined Irish, Theo and Shorty behind the end of the bar. The outlaws had put their dusters back on and were sitting at a table in the shadows. The robbers coming in the front door couldn't see them real well.

"Don't be in such a hurry," the leader said. "We want to relieve you of any cash that you have so you don't get tired carrying it up the hill."

The two railroaders pointed to the table with the outlaws and the tall one said, "We don't have any money left. Those guys at that table cleaned us out."

"Get out of here," the gunman said, turning to face the table. Two more men had come in the door behind him and fanned out on either side of the leader. Sneering, he said, "You're the men we want to talk to then. You and the barkeep. We heard tell this was the richest saloon on the river and we aim to float a little loan."

Bitter Creek leaned back in his chair. "I don't think you want to bother us or our friends here," he added nodding towards the bar. "As a matter of fact, the only floating in here tonight will be your carcass in the river if you don't leave us alone."

"Is that right?" the gang leader said. He looked at the guys on either side of him and they just laughed. "Tough guys, huh? Let's see your money on the table, now."

The roar of the guns inside that saloon was deafening. The

three outlaws gave no warning and didn't bother to let the three-man gang even pull a trigger, except in their dying moments. There was enough smoke in the room to make you think a fire had been started. The would-be robbers didn't even have enough time for surprise to show on their faces. Bitter Creek, Tulsa Jack and Charlie Pierce had a smoking gun in each hand. I never doubted that if the railroad men met these particular outlaws again under slightly different circumstances the railroaders would understand what Bitter Creek was trying to tell them.

"Let's get them out of here. They're stinking up the place," Bitter Creek said. He emptied their pockets and took their guns and holsters, tossing these to me. "Here, add these to your bar collection."

Irish and Theo helped the outlaws drag the bodies out to the river where they were unceremoniously dumped in the water and pushed off the bank.

Tulsa Jack came over to Robert and shook his hand. "I think that little soiree paid you back for the evening. I sure did enjoy holding up those railroaders tonight without a gun."

"I am impressed with the way you manipulate a deck of cards," Robert replied. "I don't think they saw a thing."

Tulsa Jack laughed. "Let them know who we were and tell them to add this money to their reward. We'll spend it for them. We'll be heading out the back door before anyone comes nosing around. We appreciate the peaceful evening."

With that the three men sauntered out the back door. Never taking their eyes off the front door as they left.

"Peaceful evening?" Robert said with wonder in his voice.

"Weren't no posses chasin' them and they made some money with very little effort," I told him. "Peaceful depends on how you look at it."

"So, you're telling me that three members of the Dalton gang just held a shootout in our saloon to keep us from being robbed. I've been in this business a long time and I've never seen anything like it," Robert said.

"You just got to catch them in a good mood," I told him. "If they had been in a hurry, they probably would have taken everything we had without askin'. As it was, you had a good night. Not as good as you would have liked. But, hey, all your body parts still work."

"It's getting rougher down here in the bottoms," he said.

"Don't fret it. When word of this gets around, guys like those three will think twice before they come in the door. Besides, we could have taken them," I said. "See, we should have kept Heaven's Gate as the saloon name. What a story this would make with our old name."

"I don't think we need any more stories about this place," he replied.

"Just think," I pointed out. "We could end up being a legend of the West. Like the James gang and the Youngers."

"And, Belle Starr?" he added.

"Yeah. Even like the Dalton gang," I replied.

"Where is Hell?

"Hell is in the Earth! Earth is the name of this planet, and when it was first made, it was a ball of fire and brimstone, or melted lava, and was prepared for the devil and his angels. . . .

"There is one other thought, or question, and that is in reference to the size of hell. The Earth is about eight thousand miles in diameter, and the crust of the Earth, upon an average, is fifty miles thick, the fifty mile of crust on each side of the Earth would make one hundred miles of crust; now, subtract one hundred from eight thousand miles, and you have the dimensions of hell, which is seven thousand and nine hundred miles of fire and brimstone."

. . . The Purcell Register, Oct. 23, 1891

Chapter 14

What's that old saying? Hell hath no Fury like a woman scorned. Robert used to tell me that every time he was about to describe Sandy's latest tirade. I have a feeling that scorning Sandy wasn't nearly as hard as Robert made it out to be. I'll give her credit though, she had him whistling Dixie through the hole left by the ring she had in his nose.

I never put much stock in prohibition. Hell, not even the United States government could keep a man away from his whiskey. But those Bible-thumping do-gooders were moving into the territory in record numbers and they were pushing mightily to ban legal drinking.

This particular fall day was like any other in Oklahoma. The farmers were coming to town with their wagons loaded with corn and cotton and broomcorn and wheat and just about anything else that they could carry. They were selling their crops in Purcell and coming back across the river to invest some of their crop money in soothing their parched throats. All that talking and haggling over prices made a man mighty thirsty.

The riverbed was alive with color. The cottonwoods and willow trees had golden yellow leaves rustling in the breeze. Up along the bluff, a few black jack oaks were turning shades of dark red and orange. The sky was just about the brightest blue you could imagine. Every morning, frost sparkled off anything that wasn't covered. You couldn't ask for a more beautiful time of the year.

However, a storm cloud on two legs was approaching. The widow of our esteemed and dearly departed revival minister - Beverly Fountains - was about to come gushing forth. She blamed us for her husband's unfortunate demise, as though we were the ones that told him to stand under a cottonwood tree in a thunderstorm. It had been almost seven months since Foghorn was reunited with his Creator in a blinding flash of glory. Now, she was about to make us think he had been raised from the dead.

About noon that day, a ruckus was being kicked off up on Depot Hill. A marching band of sorts was setting everybody's teeth on edge with a God-awful rendition of "Bringing in the Sheaves." As a matter of fact, that version sounded remarkably like a hog being rendered while it was still alive. Beverly was in the vanguard of a mob that included the band, a group of pious-looking ladies and half of Purcell. They were coming down the hill, across the railroad tracks and onto our walkway.

Luckily for us and half the dogs in the Chickasaw Nation, the walkway got overloaded and collapsed into the river just as the band was crossing over. The tuba player tried to turn back, but the weight of the horn dragged him over backwards. The sound of him hitting the water was like the whack of a good two-by-four board on the backside of a mule. He rolled over like a turtle and came up blubbering. Water came out of the tuba dousing the poor guy again. He was flapping around in the muddy water like a two-hundred pound catfish in a cattle trough. Everybody on our side of the river was rolling in laughter. You might say the band was kind of drowned out for good.

Tears were running down my face so hard, I almost missed what happened next. Mrs. Fountains was a veritable seething mountain of displeasure by this time. She looked mighty fine in her full-length, dark black dress. Her bodice was full and the corset she was wearing cinched her waist in while seemingly flaring her hips out. Her chubby little cheeks were a bright cherry red, which must have been a result of a combination of her embarrassment and her anger. The hat she wore was tilted at a crazy angle. Somebody must have snatched an eagle bald for all those feathers running down the left side of that hat.

Crowds had gathered on the porches of the Sand Bar Town saloons to watch all these shenanigans. You could hear the laughter die down one saloon at a time as they realized what had knocked her hat askew. She was glaring at us, moving her body right to left. All I could see in her left hand was a bible but my jaw dropped plumb to my chest when I saw that ax in her right hand.

Beverly Fountains only had a few followers standing around her. The band had clambered back to dry land on the Purcell side. Most of the rest of the onlookers didn't want to get their feet wet in the cause of saving Sand Bar Town. They just seated themselves up and down the riverbank for a ringside view of this carnival show.

If ever I thought old Preacher Ben's voice was loud, I was mistaken. Beverly started in with her sermon and her voice could have raised the dead in Ft. Smith, Arkansas. She pulled out the weekly edition of "The Purcell Register" and pointed to the front page.

"Here in black and white," she screeched, "is the story of this den of iniquity. 'Where is Hell?' It's right here on the sand in the South Canadian River. Never in the history of this territory has the devil gotten such a hold on the souls of so many."

She paused to point to us and I waved back because I didn't want her to think we weren't listening at least a little bit. A few of the Sand Bar Town regulars responded every now and then with an "I'll drink to that." Otherwise, we were waiting to see what happened along with everyone on the far side of the river.

"The wicked shall be turned into hell and all the nations that forget God," she read from the scripture quoted in the paper. "This newspaper asks if the Bible can tell us where hell is? We don't need the Bible to tell us where hell is. It's right here in the middle of this river and in the middle of Lexington where all those saloons and gaming houses torment lost souls every day.

"The Good Book warns us of the evil of drink," Beverly shrilled into the evening air. She turned her back on Sand Bar Town to harangue the people on the other shore. "In the book of Proverbs, chapter thirty-one, verses four through eight,

"It is not for kings, O Lemuel, it is not for kings to drink wine; nor for princes strong drink.

"Lest they drink, and forget the law," she continued, turning to point to us, her Bible open in her left hand. Her voice rose an octave or two, "and pervert the judgement of any of the afflicted.

"Give strong drink unto him that is ready to perish, and wine unto those that be heavy of heart.

"Let him drink, and forget his poverty, and remember his misery no more," Beverly said, pausing for effect.

At that moment, Sandy came out of the saloon. Her face was screwed up in an awful scowl. "What is all this damned noise? Why are you fools standing out here? Where are the customers? You can't make money standing out here. The only misery around here is listening to that caterwauling. If you ignore the old bat, she'll go back to her cave and leave us alone."

"We're being treated to a close-up view of old Ben Fountains' widow on the stump," I told her.

"Tell her to stump someplace else," Sandy retorted.

The hairs on the back of my neck stood on end as Beverly hit another shrill note. She sounded like a ninety-eight-pound woman with a two-thousand pound horse on her foot.

"Open thy mouth for the dumb in the cause of all such as are appointed to destruction," Beverly said.

Sandy came up behind Robert and pushed his shoulder.

"Get out there and shut her up."

Robert looked at her, "You've got to be joshing. They'd string me up before I could lay a hand on her."

"She's just another overrighteous Bible thumper and I don't need to listen to her," Sandy said, poking Robert in the chest.

Beverly was just about to get her second wind in the sermon. Holding up her Bible, she plunged ahead, "Proverbs, chapter twenty, verse one, says, 'Wine is a mocker, strong drink is raging; and whosoever is deceived thereby is not wise.'"

"Raging," Sandy muttered, "I'll show her raging."

"Stop her," I told Robert, "before she starts a holy war."

Sandy stopped and turned to look at me with a look that would have sent a grizzly bear into hibernation in the middle of summer. That was a cold stare.

"Don't ever get in my way again or you'll be pushing up willow trees in this riverbottom for the rest of eternity," Sandy threatened with a frosty stare.

Beverly was in fine form as she rattled on. "Isaiah, chapter five, verse eleven, 'Woe unto them that rise up early in the morning that they may follow strong drink; that continue until night, till wine inflame them.' Have you ever heard a better description of the denizens of this hell hole? The Bible has an answer for these lost souls in verse twenty.

"'Woe unto them that call evil good and good evil; that put darkness for light and light for darkness; that put bitter for sweet and sweet for bitter.'"

A wave was moving rather quickly through the Sand Bar Town crowd. It was easy to mark Sandy's progress. She swished out past the edge of the crowd. Her red satin skirt flounced around her as she trudged through the sand.

Beverly was looking towards the heavens while pointing to the ground. "In Isaiah, we know from chapter twenty-four, verse five, 'The earth is also defiled under the inhabitants thereof; because they have transgressed the laws, change the ordinance, broken the everlasting covenant.'"

Beverly's face suddenly froze in the most unsightly way out of shock at seeing Sandy standing there with her hands on her hips staring back at her.

"Will you shut up your prattle?" Sandy said in a voice that could be heard rolling off the waters.

The crowd was so silent you could hear a mouse skittering across the sand. It was just like the hush you sometimes feel just before a thunderstorm blows through.

Beverly was on a sand dune about two feet higher than where Sandy was standing. Her black outfit and black hat made her a formidable looking foe. Anybody else would have been daunt-ed. Anybody else.

"Well," sniffed Beverly, "if it isn't one of the devil's own minions, the soiled dove of the South Canadian. Here you are, dressed in red, just like the devil."

Sandy snickered. "The only thing soiled about me is my ears from having to listen to you. Here you are dressed in black, the old crow of the Canadian."

"Get thee away, you minion of Satan," Beverly shrieked.

"Your overblown bellowing has sent more men into the arms of Satan than I'll ever have a chance to do. Now get your carcass out of here and leave us alone."

Turning to her followers, Beverly pointed towards Sandy, "See what drink and carousing around and living in sin will do!"

Sandy reached up and slapped her hand away. "You point that damn thing at me again and I'll use it for your grave mark-er."

An audible gasp rippled through the crowd at hearing her language.

Beverly responded with her shrillest voice yet. "Isaiah, chap-ter five, verse fourteen, 'Therefore hell hath enlarged herself, and opened her mouth without measure; and their glory, and their multitude, and their pomp, and he that rejoiceth, shall descend into it.'"

She was very careful which direction her hands were

pointing.

"You don't know the Bible well enough to be spouting it to anyone, let alone these folks," Sandy sneered at her.

Beverly's eyebrows arched about an inch higher and her mouth drew itself into a line so straight you could have used it for a ruler. She quickly thumbed through her Bible. "Isaiah, chapter five, verse twenty-two, `Woe unto them that are might to drink wine, and men of strength to mingle strong drink.'"

Sandy snorted, "Zechariah, chapter ten, verse fifteen, `The Lord of hosts shall defend them; and they shall devour, and subdue with sling stones,'" she changed pitch, "`and they shall drink, and make a noise as through wine; and they shall be filled like bowls, and as the corners of the altar.'"

"Isaiah, chapter twenty-four, verse nine," Beverly shot back. "`They shall not drink wine with a song; strong drink shall be bitter to them that drink it."

"Zechariah, chapter ten, verse seventeen, `For how great is his goodness, and how great is his beauty, corn shall make the young men cheerful, and new wine the maids,'" Sandy added.

Another murmur rumbled through the crowd. Neither they, nor I, could believe that a saloon girl could quote chapter and verse from memory while the preacher's wife had to read the Bible.

Beverly stayed with Isaiah, "Chapter twenty-four, verse six, `Therefore hath the curse devoured the earth, and they that shall dwell therein are desolate; therefore the inhabitants of the earth are burned and few men are left."

Sandy laughed in her face. "Ecclesiastes, chapter ten, verse seven, `Go thy way, eat thy bread with joy, and drink thy wine with a merry heart; for God now accepteth thy works."

Upon hearing that, Beverly's upper lip started twitching. Quickly she thumbed to another section of the Bible, to a verse she knew well. Holding her Bible in front of her, she pointed her other hand skyward, "Romans, chapter fourteen, verse twenty-one, `It is neither good to eat flesh nor to drink wine, nor anything whereby thy brother stumbleth, or is offended, or is made weak.'"

Sandy looked at Beverly and shook her head. Very quietly, she admonished the preacher's wife. "You have read too far. You should have stopped and learned a lesson from verse ten, `But, why dost thy judge thy brother? or why dost thou set at nought thy brother? for we shall all stand before the judgement seat of Christ.'"

Sandy had finally achieved her aim. Beverly shut up.

Suddenly, a sound drifted from one of the tents near the edge of saloon row. One of the customers had chosen the most inopportune moment to refill his glass from the keg on the bar. The sloshing of the beer filling the glass caused something to snap in Beverly. She reached behind her and grabbed the axe, swinging it around to her front. The movement caught Sandy offguard and she stumbled backwards in the sand.

Holding the axe about waist high, Beverly headed for the tent. The crowd was so shocked to see her head their way, they stood there with their mouths agape while she plowed right through them. The man with the beer saw her coming with that axe and started shaking so bad he spilled beer all over himself and anyone else within a ten-foot radius. Not noticing the man at all, Beverly stopped long enough to grab the axe handle in both hands. Then, she reared back and took a swing at the keg. The sound of the axe clanging off the wood brought a couple of saloonkeepers out of their shock.

The first blow knocked the keg off the bar, but did little damage. As she swung the axe over her head this time, a low moan started from the men closest to the bar. The splintering of the end panel on the keg could be heard from one end of Sand Bar Town to the other. The beer began pouring out, darkening the sand.

Since Beverly had so kindly started her sermon calling Sand Bar Town hell on earth, she was about to find out what it was going to be like when all hell did break out.

The saloon owner screamed at Beverly as she stood over the

keg trying to remove the axe. The customers from the other saloons were pushing and shoving to get a better view of the brouhaha. Beverly started screaming back at the guy who was yelling at her. Her hat was shoved down over her eyes, so she had a hard time seeing what was going on around her.

She finally freed the axe and made a sashay toward the liquor bottles at the back of the bar. That was too much for the saloon-keeper. He grabbed the axe handle up near the head and jerked Beverly around. They danced around in a circle while each one tried to wrench the axe free. When she saw she couldn't break his grip, Beverly dropped the handle and went for the poor guy's throat instead. She bowled him over and they rolled around on the sawdust floor until a half dozen guys picked her up and headed for the door. She was kicking and twisting something fierce. Her scream reached a pitch never before heard or made by man nor beast. With her set of lungs, she could have put a whole battalion of Rebels to shame when it came to yelling.

The six men stumbled across the sand and were finally able to toss her in the river. She sat up, her wet hat and feathers bedraggled. She was quiet for maybe two seconds while she spluttered herself back to life.

"Where's the sheriff? Where are the U.S. marshals? Don't just stand there gawking, somebody get the law down here," she yelled at the people on the Purcell side of the river. Looking back at us, she shook her fist, "I'm not through with you yet. I'll live to see the day Sand Bar Town is forever removed from the face of the earth."

"Yeah, well, it won't be tonight, lady," the saloonkeeper said. "You ain't welcome here. If we see you comin' this way again with an axe in your hand, we'll use it on you. Get on up to Purcell and leave us alone. Better yet, go stand on the railroad tracks and let us know when the next train comes through."

Two or three men from the band on the Purcell side waded quickly into the river and lifted Beverly up to carry her back across. They landed her on her feet and spent the next few minutes fighting her up the bank of the river. She kept trying to turn back, but they kept firm hands on her elbows. I couldn't hear what she was saying and was damn glad I couldn't.

By the time she was halfway up Depot Hill, everyone in Sand Bar Town was back in their favorite spots by the bars. Sandy was slumped in her favorite seat near the front door, waiting impatiently for her next customer. She kept muttering something about business going to hell in a hand basket. Robert sat down at the table, a kind of awe on his face. I stood at the bar pouring drinks.

"How did you know all those verses from the Bible?" he asked her.

She gave him a sideways glance. "I learned it growing up," she replied tersely.

"But you didn't even hesitate. I mean, you knew every verse you quoted and exactly where she was in the Bible."

"Yep."

"How?"

"All my life, I had to listen to that stuff being forced down my throat by my old man. Every time I turned around, he was quoting the Bible, telling me I was a bad girl just before he beat the stuffing out of me. I had to learn the Bible just to defend myself so I wouldn't go crazy."

"Amazing," Robert said.

"Don't ever try to argue the Bible with me. And don't try to use it to shame me into anything," she said vehemently.

"Didn't your father know the Bible better than that?" he asked.

"Look, my old man was a Baptist preacher just like that old windbag's recently departed. He never even tried to brace me when I left home. There's a reason they call it the Good Book, but he didn't bring that up very often. The Bible I carry with me is a lot more personal than hers."

"Amen," I said.

"Dr. Ballard is in receipt of a letter from the Oklahoma Board of Health, saying the examiner for Cleveland County, Dr. Chas. F. Waldron, will meet the physicians of this section who wish to comply with the law regulating the practice of medicine in Oklahoma at any time in the near future which they may designate. Under the laws of that territory, all physicians who desire to practice within its boundaries must either stand examination before the Board of Health, or register their diploma."

. . . The Purcell Register, Aug. 14, 1891

Chapter 15

The Twin Territories were the place where a man could leave his past behind and start all over, two or three times if he was lucky. One of the reasons my brother and I came here from Kansas was to put some hard times and hardscrabble behind us. I was so tired of harvesting more rocks than crops, I was ready to move when Linc made the suggestion. I had heard that in Oklahoma the soil was so rich that fence posts would take root and grow. Anything had to be better than what we were doing in southeast Kansas.

Of course, every cloud has a silver lining and every silver lining has a cloud, or something to that effect. The move to Indian Territory was great for me, what with the land run, the saloon and the corn liquor. And, for awhile, Linc was doing a booming business as a doctor. He even opened an apothecary shop over in Barnett in the Pottawottamie country. The land rush just plumb ruined that part of the territories. What with all the new people and more white folks in the middle of Hell's Fringe. And, all those folks meant more lawmen and more judges and more interference from these so-called law-abiding folks.

Luckily, most of the law-abiding citizens of Oklahoma Territory in the Lexington area were too busy making a profit out of illegally selling booze to the Indians to worry about us folks in the middle of the river. Linc just wasn't as lucky. By the

middle of 1892, the liquor business was running fairly smoothly. You no longer needed a prescription to buy alcohol and that
had cut down our need for Linc. There was an occasional bullet
wound or knife cut that he helped fix.

He kept busy over in the Pottawotamie country, though,
mending broken bones and handing out doses of medicine to
people out in the country. There weren't a lot of doctors in that
region and none of them was willing to run a circuit through the
country on a regular basis. I have no idea why he liked people
doctoring so much, but he took to medicine like a duck takes to
water. I guess he got it from our mother. He used to sit for
hours and listen to her talk about what she did as a midwife. I
never did understand why he was so fascinated with it. Listening
to that stuff just made me sick.

Sometimes our middle of the week business wasn't as active
as we would have liked. Harvest time was even slower because
all the farmhands were too damn busy during the day and too
damned tired at night to do much of anything. Late August in
Indian Territory always gave a whole new meaning to wishing for
a cold day in hell. The hot weather was good for drying out the
corn but it left a lot to be desired when it came to trying to stay
cool. Being down in the riverbottom helped some, although by
this time of year, the South Canadian River had disappeared into
the sand. It was the one time of the year when quicksand was
not a problem. You could walk across the sand river just about
anywhere.

Sandy was sitting on the front porch waving a fan in front of
her face, complaining about her heat rash and pointing out some
of the more unusual patterns in the mirages that were radiating
off the hot sand.

"Ooh, look at that one," she said, pointing off to the north
upriver. "It looks like some damn giant stringbean riding a
giraffe."

A few minutes later she came in the front door. "I think I'll
go into Lexington and do some shopping. That mirage turned

into an ass riding a mule. Your fool brother is coming. I can't take two Swedens in the same building at the same time."

"Ahh," I replied, "can't stand to be in the presence of such greatness. Well, you don't know what you're missin'."

"Yeah, well, that's when ignorance is bliss. I'll leave now and enjoy my bliss."

About the time the back door closed, the front door opened and Linc walked in. "Welcome, brother. Haven't seen you in awhile. How's the doctorin' business?"

"Couldn't be better. There's sick people all over the place and most of them can't find a doctor willing to travel 20 miles to their farms. Being a country doctor does have its benefits."

He moved over to the end of the bar and stood with his hands on his hips, staring out the window. He was wearing a flat-crowned hat with a narrow brim. He looked more like a preacher than a doctor. His chin was covered with a goatee and he had a pair of reading glasses draped across his nose. A leather cord attached to the right side of the glasses rim was wrapped around a button on his vest pocket. The pinstripe suit he had on was a little baggy and had a few dark spots from sweat stains and all the riding he had been doing on his horse.

"I remember that look on your face," I told him. "You didn't come here for a friendly palaver. What's put a burr under your saddle?"

He turned to look at me. Reaching up, he took his glasses off and slid them into his vest pocket. The bright sunlight from the window gave him a harsh look. He took a newspaper clipping out of his pocket and flipped in on the bar.

"Did you see that? It was in the paper not too long ago."

"So? Go take your doctor's test or get some school to send you a certificate. Hell, I can find somebody around here that probably has an old certificate you can use," I said with a little laugh.

He raised his right eyebrow. "It isn't funny. I don't need any damned commission telling me how to do my job. This place is just getting too damned civilized."

"Let me see. The last time I heard that was down in Wynnewood while you were workin' for the railroad. The time before that you were in Kansas. Neosho Springs wasn't it? Too damned many people leads to too much trouble for you. We've moved from Michigan to Kansas to the territory. Where else do you plan on goin'?"

"As far as it takes."

"What does Martha say about another move?"

"Not much. I haven't told her I'm even thinking about leaving. She likes the place where we're living."

"Something has changed. You don't usually let a few laws bother you."

Linc rubbed his chin and looked at me with a wistful expression. He glanced back out the window. "Well, I met a seamstress over around Barnett, and, well, she stayed with us awhile. And, well, she treats me just like a doctor. Calls me doctor. She knows I'm a doctor. And, well, ..."

"The rest of us still think you're a horse doctor," I said, "is that what's botherin' you?"

"I've spent a lot of time building up my practice. A lot of people around here depend on me. All I've done for you is pull bullets and arrows out of some fool's rear end or give out some damn fake prescriptions so you can get rid of that poison you call whiskey. That's no way for a doctor to do his work."

"Well, I'll be hornswoggled. Now, let me get this straight," I said, not quite believing what I was hearing. I knew Linc had the wanderlust, but I never thought it was this bad. "You're tellin' me that you're gettin' ready to run off and leave your wife and kids just because some fool woman thinks you're a doctor. The reason we came here was because some damn fool company thought you stole drugs in your store in Kansas and you wanted to start over. I can't remember why we moved to Kansas. I think I like my little patch of South Canadian sand. I'm not pullin' up stakes again on some fool's errand."

He looked at me with a skeptical expression on his face. "I am not asking you to come with me. I don't need you around to remind me of all the times we've had to skedaddle before the footsteps got too close. No. Regardless of what you think of me, you're about the only one in the territory I can talk to. I know you won't tell anybody else. I've just been thinking about this for awhile. I just wanted to see how you'd react."

"What do you want me to do? You're my brother. There isn't anywhere we haven't been together. I like this country. It's done right by me. Like I said, I think my roots have sunk and I'm goin' to stay."

Linc started laughing. "You think this godforsaken place is where you want to call home? Haven't I taught you anything over the years? You stay too long in one place and you get stale. That isn't grass growing under your feet. It's green mold. I've told you over and over. You can't hit a fast moving target."

"Now I remember why we left Michigan. Let me see, Michigan was godforsaken because any place where you had to work that hard couldn't be anywhere close to paradise. We left Kansas because that godforsaken state had ground so hard that a plow and a brace of oxen couldn't even leave a scratch. I don't even want to know why this place is godforsaken. Besides, we got so many preachers comin' down here to save us, God can't have given up on us that quickly."

"Go ahead. Make fun of me. This is serious business. I can't live somewhere where I'm not appreciated."

"Oh, hell, I appreciate you. You've come in handy in a lot of tight scrapes. You know, there's not a single person ever found us after we ran one of our scams. There's been two or three of those railroaders we worked on a couple of years ago come through here and they didn't recognize me at all. Those foot-steps you been hearin' all these years is just our old man comin' after us with a switch, yellin' at you to get your lazy ass in gear and get some work done. I can't hear him any more. I like the view from behind the bar."

"That's always been your trouble, D.W. You have no ambition. You'll settle for some hell hole that smells like stale whiskey and rotten tobacco."

"Smells good, don't it?"

"No. It stinks. I don't know why I bother talking to you."

"Because nobody else will listen. And those that think they know you would be plumb shocked at what you're wantin' to do. I'm the only one that's used to you. Even your latest wife doesn't know what to expect. You're right. I ain't goin' to tell her neither. Want a drink?"

"Sure. Why not? I'll let you poison me one more time."

"You love this stuff. I've seen you pass up some of that pure Kentucky whiskey just for a whiff of my bottled best."

"You know you have to drink this stuff fast before it etches the glass. The term rotgut came from a bottle of your finest. I have watched you make this lousy whiskey for years and this is by far the best you've ever made. It does have a unique taste that actually makes this stuff taste good. How do you do it?"

I pursed my lips and looked at him slightly askance. "I have a secret ingredient."

That made him laugh even louder.

"Just for that. I'll keep it to myself."

"The last time you had a secret, I damn near got my head blown off by some freak of nature that thought you had put a curse on him. You can't expect me to believe that this secret won't kill me since you didn't get it done the first time."

"How was I supposed to know that some old hermit out in the woods was a crazy old hunchback? I almost had that whole town ready to buy those magic bags. I didn't think you'd ever get your voice back after he tried to drive that wooden stake through your bread basket. I don't know where he heard that old wives' tale."

"So, D.W., what's in this stuff?"

"Oh, no, you don't. That flankin' movement won't work this time."

"Speaking of flanking movements, do you remember the time that troop of cavalry got into your still? You'd just put something in it to clean it. Lord, I've never seen anyone as sick as those men were. For the first twenty minutes or so, they were bragging about how good it tasted and who could drink the most. Whatever they threw up looked like the rusted inside of your still. You came up yelling at them to get away from the still."

"Yeah. And the ones that could still stand straight up drew their sabers and came hightailin' it after me. Not one of my better moments."

"I can't remember you ever moving quite so fast. What was it? Five miles from town. You were on foot and they were trying to run and shoot with one hand and promising to stick you like a roasting pig with the other hand. It's a good thing they were so sick," Linc remembered, laughing so hard he spilled his drink. "I had just pulled up in my buggy and you came past like somebody had shot you out of a cannon. It's a good thing I had a doctor's bag back then. The soldiers that were left were weaving in the saddle pretty badly by the time they reached town. It wasn't hard to get them off the street so I could look after them. That's one debt you still haven't repaid."

"Now wait just a minute. I remember the time you got into the snake oil business and almost got strung up when the mayor's wife got so drunk from the medicine that she took her clothes off in front of the hotel because she was so hot. You could hear that corset pop a half a mile away. As I recall, you had to stay the night in my freight wagon, at no extra cost, I remind you, so's you'd still have your head attached the next day. Seems to me we're even on that score."

"Hold on, hold on. Do you remember the first time you tried that Running Bear scam? That old Indian you bribed with a bottle of your rotgut was so drunk, he couldn't even stay in the saddle, let alone claim the money on the blanket."

I looked hurt. "That's still a good one. I never made that

mistake again. You cain't trust those real Indians."

"Let me see, that was an immigrant train passing through as I recall. Those greenhorns were so scared of that drunk Indian that they peed in their pants on the spot. You got greedy and went after the blanket. Not everybody was bothered by the wild heathen. That's the only time I've ever had to pull any lead out of you."

"I may not be good," I said, "but I am a fast learner."

"So, for all those times I threw in with you on that scam, you can at least tell me what's in this whiskey."

The bar had been quiet most of the afternoon. The only noise you could hear was the buzzing of the flies as they flitted from spot to spot. I walked to the back room and made sure Robert was still gone and Sandy wasn't back yet. I went to the front door and checked the porch and closed the door. I went back to the bar and leaned close to Linc's ear.

"You got to promise me you won't let out a peep about this. I could be ruined if any of this got out," I whispered.

"You think I'm off my rocker. Look at you. You act as though this is the worst thing you've ever done. We've just gone over half the crimes we ever committed in voices anybody in tent town could hear. Now, you want to whisper."

"Look, Linc, it ain't about breakin' the law. This could be embarrassin'. I've built up a good followin' and if word of this spreads, I'll be the laughin' stock of the territory whether the liquor tastes good or not."

"You are really serious, aren't you? What in the hell could you have put in your still that would be so silly? You must have really given the devil his due on this one. Let me guess, this really is sheep dip," he said, laughing.

"All right, if you're gonna make fun of me before I even tell you, then I'll just keep it to myself."

"Okay. Okay. I'll control myself. I'm laughing because there's nothing else we've ever done that has had you so buffaloed. If you haven't been embarrassed by the rest of these things, I can't imagine what would cause you to act like this."

I headed for the windows for one more look around before I went behind the bar. I reached down and took out a jar filled with little orange-brown balls. I rolled a couple of them across to Linc. He picked one up and looked at it. Sniffed it. His frown was so deep it looked like someone had drawn some black lines between his eyebrows. They're too small for oranges. Too round for carrots. Don't look like potatoes or onions. What are they?"

"Persimmons," I whispered.

"What? Did you say per. . . ."

He got that out before I could get my hand over his mouth. His eyes were as round as a fifty-cent piece. "I told you to keep it down. You can't yell it all over the valley."

Slowly, he removed my hand from his mouth. In a lower tone, he said, "Persimmons?"

"Exactly. I dry them out, drop a couple of them in the mash and let the still take its course."

"How in the hell did you ever think to try this?"

"Well, there's so many persimmon trees around here I put my still up in the middle of a grove one time. It was late in the fall and I was tryin' to get the tube attached to the top of the pot before I put it on the fire. While I was doin' that, a few persimmons dropped into the pot and I couldn't fish them all out. So I said the hell with it and started cookin' the mash. I got some of the sweetest tastin' booze I had ever made. I experimented a bit and finally found that two dried persimmons made the best flavor. Nobody else has come close to makin' theirs taste like mine and I'd like to keep it that way."

He laughed again. "I don't know whether to believe you or not. Sometimes I think you do this just to irritate me."

"Now, big brother, this is just one of those lucky breaks that I've stumbled upon. There's no sense in makin' a big deal out of this. You keep quiet about this and I'll keep quiet about yours."

"I thought that was the way we always did business, D.W.,"
Linc said. "Well, you're right. Now that I know what's in this
stuff, it doesn't taste nearly as good. Adios."

I watched him walk out into the late afternoon sun. I did-
n't think about it at that moment, but I had never heard him say
"Adios" before. It was always, "I'll see you in a month of
Sundays" or "Drop in and see us sometime."

A couple of weeks later, two of his oldest sons came in and
asked if I had seen him lately. I said, no, he came in and had a
drink awhile ago. I asked them how come they were looking for
him. Curtis told me that they had come to town a week ago and
gone into Purcell on business. Curtis went one way and Linc the
other. When it came time to go home, Linc was nowhere to be
found. After asking around, he traced him to the train station
where Linc had bought a ticket to Dallas.

I told him that I had no idea Linc was thinking about going
to Texas. He hadn't said a thing about that. That's when I
remembered what he had said. After the boys left, I poured
myself a drink and toasted Linc. I wished him luck wherever he
was headed. He had an itch to move on and he finally scratched
it. I never saw him again.

"The Canadian is on another rampage, on Wednesday night it took the greatest rise it has had this season. Thursday morning the last house on the sand bar, which was built for a dance hall, was washed away and after floating some distance down the stream was broken up by the angry waves, disappearing entirely."
. . . The Purcell Register, June 19, 1891

Chapter 16

The Floating Palace Saloon was still doing a booming business especially in the heat of the summertime. For some reason, our customers fully believed that the only way to break the heat was to come in out of the sun and have a drink or two. We had found an added benefit to having a saloon in the riverbottom. You could put the beer in a hole under the saloon and the wet sand kept it at a nice cool temperature.

This had been a very wet year in the territories. After watching the Heaven's Gate Saloon wash down the river, Robert and Sandy and I were always a little bit nervous when a storm was brewing off to the northwest. Those fast-moving fronts that dropped a few tornadoes, a little hail and even less rain weren't too bad. But those slow-moving thunderstorms that opened up the heavens with a frog-strangling, gully-washing torrent of rain were the worst kind.

Only three weeks after the Floating Palace was finished, a good rain raised the river up a mite. I think the local newspaper described the event as "The Canadian is on a big rampage and the sand-bar town is an excellent habitation for ducks." That was the strangest feeling of all when that saloon began to float. One second you were on solid ground and the next you were flat on your backside as the barge was lifted out of the sand and moved down river in spurts and starts.

In the middle of all this came a whooping and hollering outside the back door. A couple of cowhands threw some loops around the hitching post on the back porch. I could feel the

135

saloon swinging around in the swirling water until the cowboys hauled us closer to shore.

I'll give old Pegleg Pete his due. The boat, er, saloon held together real well. It took three teams of mules and a brace of oxen to move it back into position. From that time on, the first drink of the evening was always free for those two cowboys. Now, really, I couldn't give them free drinks all the time, I'd have been in the poor house.

We did move the saloon back a few yards and up a taller sand dune after that. Since Sand Bar Town was well established, being the closest saloon to the bridge didn't matter so much anymore. Luckily for us, that was a good move. Come early June, the heavens opened up again. I rode this one out in the saloon but it was close. When the water started going down, I pulled a copy of that rag from Purcell out of the water. Sure enough, they were right on the ball.

"The Canadian is gloriously full to-day, extending from bank to bank and making a stream about one and one-half miles wide. The mail from Lexington has been delayed considerably by this latest freak of the uncertain stream. From the quantity and variety of the driftwood going down the Canadian, the old stream is sweeping things all along. It is reported that one man has fished out a good wagon, catching the several parts at different times, but we haven't seen the wagon."

That was on June 5. All that water soaked into the ground and the red clay soil was slicker than a saloon floor in a spitting contest. We were ready for it to dry out. By the end of August, every man, woman, child and horned toad in the country would be praying for a good rain.

"D.W.," yelled Robert from the front porch, "get out here. Pronto."

I put down the cloth I was polishing the glasses with and came out to see what had his bowels in an uproar.

"I could have sworn the water level was going down. Now look."

Sure enough, the water seemed to be rising again. "I don't know, maybe a dam broke upstream somewhere."

A few minutes later, a buggy came tearing down the hill from Purcell. Sandy was whipping that poor horse like a house fire in a high wind. She jerked the reins back, skittering the rear end of the carriage around. "We're in for it now," she said, breathlessly. There's another storm coming and there's a wave of water ahead of it. It's already washed out a bridge upriver. Help me load up and get out of here."

That was the only time in my life I ever saw Sandy Peaks scared. She rushed in and out of the saloon with her arms full of bottles and dresses and anything else she could get her hands on. And, she never stopped talking.

"I knew better than to get involved in a deal like this. I can't swim. Did you know that I can't swim? What would happen if I got caught in the middle of the river in high water? I tell you what would happen, I would become fish food."

"You mean you'd give some poor fish indigestion," I said, trying to lighten her mood. She didn't even rise to the bait.

"Robert, did I ever tell you the reason I was going to Tucson? Well, it was because it's dry in Arizona. They have a desert out there. Not a drop of water unless it comes out of a well. Can you imagine never having to worry about drowning? That sounds so nice. If I ever see that damned stagecoach driver again, I'll drown him. That's everything. Let's go."

She didn't wait for an answer. The buggy jumped as the horse bolted towards Lexington and safety. The breaking of glass could be heard clearly across the riverbottom.

"Well, I'm glad she's yours," I said. "Why don't you go upriver and tell the boys and I'll go downriver. It's awfully quiet along here. I have a feelin' all the birds and animals have headed for higher ground too."

"I do believe you're right. Look. The water's come up another half foot while we were standing here loading the buggy."

That gave us a little impetus to get moving. I walked into the Sand Bar Saloon and was immediately disappointed. The Three Bucketeers had abandoned my saloon for a cheaper brand of whiskey.

"Hey, Irish," Theo mumbled. "We're in the wrong saloon. Let's go."

"What the hell are you blabberin' about?" Shorty asked.

"There goes the neighborhood," Irish said. "I thought we'd given you up as a bad habit."

"What did I do to you three? You were my best customers."

"How can you call us that?" Theo muttered. "The only time we ever saw you, you was insultin' us callin' us the Three Bucketeers. Why in the hell did you call us that?"

"Well, because you three was always together and you reminded me of the Three Musketeers. Instead of muskets, you guys were always involved in buckets of beer. You know, the Three Bucketeers. One for all and all for one and drinks all around."

"Best customers, hell," Irish said, his dander up. "We heard about you givin' those free drinks to those cowboys. Every time they come in. Do you know how much money we could have saved? How much more whiskey we could have downed? You're the worst blackguard in the valley."

"Boy, I'd have to go some to live up to that reputation. Besides, if the three of you were ever sober enough to ride a horse you could save the saloon. You do that and I'll give you a free drink of whiskey and a beer. Oh, damn, I forgot about the beer. Look, Tom," I told the bartender. "You need to get these guys out of here and head for the hills. They got a wire over at the train station that a flood is headed this way and that it had already washed out a bridge upstream. You can see the clouds building off to the northwest now."

"Sure. Sure," Tom said. "I'll take care of my customers. You go find your own."

"Hey, Tom. I've never lied to you and I sure as hell wouldn't lie about something like this. We've already cleaned out our saloon and packed it in to Lexington. You can see the water rising now. That's not a good sign. Listen. My barge is the best one built along here and we're goin' into town. Come on. I'll help you."

"That's all right," Shorty said. "We'll take care of Tom's liquor supply."

"We can float downstream on the empty beer kegs," Irish cackled. "Besides, this here Ark has a charmed life."

"It's going to have to be down right blessed if it's going to survive this one." They were all laughing as I left them there, shaking my head in disgust. I went next door to the First Chance and Last Chance Saloon and got pretty much the same reception. They wouldn't leave until Tom left. By the time I got back to the Floating Palace, the glory hole where we kept the beer kegs was full. A couple of the barrels had floated out from under the barge, but the water wasn't deep enough for them to float away. Even I was worried by this time. I found a rope and looped it around the beer barrels. By the time I was done with that, I could float them across the sand. I took my little herd and started wading towards shore. By the time I reached the foot of Main Street in Lexington, I could hear the Floating Palace start to creak and groan. And, I knew then those guys in the Ark were in trouble.

Robert came back down the street with the buggy and helped me load up the beer. "Did you get the rest of them out?" I asked.

"Yeah. It didn't take much to convince the guys in the tents. After that flood two weeks ago, they were gone in the blink of an eye."

"Well, I wasn't so lucky. Theo, Shorty and Irish are in Tom's saloon and they were too damned drunk to believe me."

A long groan wafted across the waters. Robert and I watched the Floating Palace move slowly under the force of the water. The saloon creaked and moved downstream, bumping the Ark before sliding out into the river. The Floating Palace was out of sight in a few minutes. After the Ark was bumped, the four men came out the back door and started yelling their fool heads off.

"Damn. I was afraid of that."

Robert and I started running down the riverbank until we were even with the saloon. Even though this part of the river was the shallowest part of the riverbed, there was still a lot of swirling water between us and the saloon. A tree trunk came gliding out of the gloom, ramming the side of the saloon and they started screaming even louder. The late afternoon sun was now hidden by the oncoming clouds and a semi-dark gloom settled over the river.

A farmer with a big-footed plow horse had come down to the river to see what all the commotion was about. I recognized him as Bob Scott.

"Hey, Bob. The river's rising fast and they're trapped out there in that saloon."

He looked at the river and the distance and then back at that huge old horse. "I'll go get 'em."

That big old horse was amazing. The water didn't seem to bother it or slow it down in the least. He headed straight to the First Chance and Last Chance Saloon. He loaded two men behind him and came back to shore. He left them on high ground and went back for the other one. This one wasn't so lucky. He was too drunk to stay on behind the farmer. He slid off behind the horse and made a futile grab for the tail before the muddy water swept him away. I could see Bob shake his head and turn back to the Ark. After what seemed like a long time and after an argument we could hear from shore, he turned back and headed to the riverbank. He dropped off Tom and Theo and went back for one last trip. By this time it was almost dark and the Ark was the only building left on the sand bar.

"What the hell were you arguin' about out there?" I asked Theo. "I swear you guys don't have sense enough to pour piss out of a boot."

"They forced me up onto that horse. We drew straws and I won. Then they picked me up and threw me on that damned horse. I should be out there and Irish should be here on dry ground."

At that moment, a loud crack split the evening air. I could see Bob with Shorty up behind him. The front of the Sand Bar Saloon was twisting in the flood waters and the rest of the saloon was rapidly collapsing. The horse was shying away from the noise of the collapsing building. As the farmer reached out to grab Irish's hand, the saloon tore away in the churning water. In a lightning flash, the saloon and the big, ruddy Irishman were gone. How that horse made it back to the riverbank, I'll never know.

I sat down hard on the ground and started crying. Theo had fainted. I heard the clomp of the horse's hooves on the bank and Shorty dropped down beside me.

"He's gone. Poof. No more. Two more inches and he'd have been safe. Damned fool Irishman," Shorty said.

A slow rain began to fall as the last light faded. The water was still inching up the riverbank as we sat there in the coming night. I couldn't believe that the whole Sand Bar Town and two men were gone.

"I guess we'll have to have a wake for him. That's the way I know he'd want to go. Drinks are on me. I hope he catches up with the Floatin' Palace and gets a free ride into paradise," I said.

"Hell, if he catches up with any saloon, he'll be in paradise. He won't need to go there," Shorty replied. "If we hadn't been arguin' out there on who was goin' first and who was goin' last, we'd had more time to get out of that saloon."

"Oh, hell," I said, "if I'd taken a horsewhip to you and run you out of that saloon when I came by, everyone would be alive."

"What a way to go," Shorty wailed. "Irish never did like to cut his whiskey with water and the water finally got him before the whiskey did."

Robert reached down and grabbed me under my arms from

142

behind and tried to lift me. "C'mon. It's dark. It's raining. The saloon is gone and there's nothing more you can do."

I kind of stumbled to my feet. "But, you don't realize. We just lost one of our best customers," I whined.

"No," he replied, "you lost one of your best customers. He never pulled a chair up to a poker table the whole time I knew him. At least I don't have to listen to anymore godawful renditions of 'My Wild Irish Rose.' I swear he ran off more of my gambling friends than your bad whiskey."

"That's a hell of a way to talk about the recently departed. What are you thinkin' about?"

"I'm trying not to think," Robert said. "That could have been us out there. If Sandy hadn't been so damned scared, we never would have believed her."

"I guess we owe her one," I mumbled. "She can have a drink on the house. If we ever get a house back."

"That's something we're going to have to talk about," he added. "We can't afford to build another boat like that. It was the best money can buy and still the river took it away."

About that time, Theo rolled over and came awake. He ran over to Shorty and grabbed his sleeve. "Where's Irish? That was the worst drunk I've ever had. I had a nightmare that Irish was swept away by the river."

Shorty looked his friend in the eye. "You weren't drunk enough. That was no nightmare. He's gone on his way to the Gulf of Mexico. Or, at least his body is."

Even with the feeble light from the kerosene lanterns in the windows of the houses along the street, I could see Theo's face turn a lighter shade of white. If he had any blood flowing through the veins in his face, I sure couldn't see it. He was flat sober before we reached Main Street. We headed for the hotel. Theo didn't say a word. He just sat in the lobby watching the door. I guess he expected Irish to come roaring back through there any moment.

Theo and Shorty were gone the next morning when I got up.

I didn't have any idea where they had gone, but I had an idea they headed downriver to see if some Irish saint had produced a miracle. The Irish gods were not smiling that night.

It took nearly a week for the waters to drop low enough to get back across the river to Purcell. I spent most of my time trying to find what was left of my still. The high water had filled the ravine where it was hidden and most of it had joined the Floating Palace somewhere south and east of Purcell.

The best news that came out of this flood is that the Floating Palace did float. It ended up half buried in some quicksand about ten miles downstream. We were lucky that someone who knew us found it before all those sod-busting scavengers could break it up for matchsticks. I was able to talk Robert into a salvage operation. It ended up being considerably cheaper than building a new one. The day we floated it back into dry dock near Lexington, you could hear the cheers from the drinkers and the groans from the prohibitionists drifting down Depot Hill.

From that moment on, the Floating Palace always stopped for a few minutes of silence on June 19. Shorty always came around for a couple of drinks at the anniversary of the "Great Flood." Theo never touched another drop of liquor. Last I heard, he was working a farm in the Texas Panhandle where everything was dry.

Except for the clinking of glasses, the only sound you could hear during the yearly wake was someone singing, "My Wild Irish Rose."

"Dr. Mock Turtle, of the Cherokee tribe, but who spends his time traveling around selling Indian medicines, is here this week, visiting relatives in this vicinity."

. . . The Purcell Register, Oct. 16, 1891

Chapter 17

Some people seemed to think that the Indians were savages and uncivilized. There were a few folks that never did seem to realize how intelligent those Indians were. And, boy, it didn't take them long to learn the white man's ways. As anyone who has ever traded horses with an Indian can attest, the inscrutable savage can be as tricky and deceitful as any white man ever born. And these Indians in the five civilized tribes have had 60 years to learn from some of the worst white men in the country.

They believed in fighting for what the U.S. government had given them in exchange for the rest of the country. Don't forget, a lot of these Indians owned slaves and fought in their own brand of Civil War in Indian Territory. Since Kansas, Missouri, Arkansas, Texas and Colorado were now states with their own laws and lawmen, Oklahoma and Indian Territories were the sanctuaries for some of the most lethal outlaws anywhere in the country. Every cheat, con man and whiskey peddler in a thousand-mile radius at one time or another plied their trade in the territories. Like I said, those Indians learned fast.

There's something about whiskey and Indians that never seemed to mix well. From the time the territory was formed, the one federal rule that was always in effect was, "Don't sell whiskey to the Indians." And, of course, there were more whiskey peddlers hauled into Ft. Smith court than murderers or robbers. All those woods and gullies made great hiding places for stills. And, the Indians never missed a thing in their country. They were a lot sharper than some of the deputy marshals sent out to corral the bad guys.

Late fall was a kind of lazy time in the territories. The crops

144

were all in and there wasn't much for the farmers to do except
work on their equipment and get ready for the coming spring.
The leaves were off the trees and the grass was a dingy yellow.
The temperatures were cold with frost out almost every morning. The only way to stay warm was to get in out of the wind.

I was cleaning up the bar getting ready for the day's business
when I heard a series of thumps along the south side of the
saloon. I had no idea what was going on, but I was going to find
out. I pulled out the shotgun and went out the back door and
around the side of the saloon. Holding the shotgun about hip
level as I rounded the corner, I saw George Big Tree leaning
against the side of the saloon wrapped in a blanket.

"Are you going squirrel hunting?" he asked me, without
opening his eyes.

"No. I think I'm goin' to shoot me a big turkey, though."

"Gobble, gobble."

I took the shotgun back inside and brought a chair back and
plunked down next to him. "I haven't seen you in awhile."

"I thought it was time for another free drink."

"When did I ever do a thing like that?" I said.

"The day of the land run," he replied. "You were all philo-
sophical and morose."

"Mo what?"

"Morose. You know, gloomy, glum. The exact opposite of
all those people charging across the river," George said.

"Well, your Cherokee brethren are doin' it again. That must
be why you're here again. I take it you were back in Washington
tryin' to stop them from openin' the Cherokee Outlet."

"Those greedy whites won out again. Over six-and-a-half
million acres and the government pushed them into selling it for
a dollar and twenty-five cents an acre. The white man is never
satisfied with what he has. Always he wants more."

"Maybe that's the problem with you Indians. You don't
know what you want and you keep givin' away what you got."

"This is a nice place to while away the day. Warm sun. This

looks like a new saloon."

"It is. This one floats. It's built on a barge so we don't lose it in a flood. Is that a new blanket?"

"Sure is," he said as he leaned forward and removed the blanket. It was solid red except for a white buffalo in the middle. "I understand your old black blanket did survive one of the times the river was running full."

"The river took the blanket and one of my competitor's with it. That was the end of the First Chance and Last Chance Saloon. You might say it really was their last chance. They've got a new copy of 'Custer's Last Stand' in the Sand Bar Saloon. I'm surprised you didn't pull up alongside their place."

"They don't have a nice railing like this so you can prop up your feet. Otherwise I'd have to get sand all over everything," George laughed.

"You're dressed like an Indian, so you must be hidin' from somebody. There's nothin' down here in the river bottom to see."

"Not so. It's a different perspective. I still spend a lot of time on Red Hill. I came down here to see what life in Oklahoma is like. Besides that wind up there today is bitter."

"Boy, talk about gloom and doom. You sound like you hear the horns of Jericho and your walls are about to come tumblin' down."

He shaded his eyes and looked at me. "When I was a boy, I could hunt up and down any of these creeks and rivers and would never be bothered. Now, I have trouble walking down the sidewalk in Purcell. Some overbearing white man would rather I walk in the dust than share a sidewalk with him in my own nation. Soon there will be a Chickasaw Nation in name only. That will be a sad time."

"It's progress."

"White man's progress. If it was left up to the Indian, there would be no fences and there would be no farms on the plains. You crazy white men are up there burning thousands of acres in the Cherokee Outlet so the cattlemen won't use it. That kind of idiocy then gets the whites in Washington to force the Cherokees to sell what was given to them forever in a treaty. Only this time, there is no other place to send the Indians. At least we won't have a `Trail of Tears' this time."

"Why do I have the feelin' that you're about to change the subject again?"

"Ahh, Mr. Sweden, you can tell my passion sometimes gets the better of me when I'm talking about Indian affairs. I just came down here to sit in the sunshine and dream of better days."

I pointed to a couple of wagons that were pulling across the ford. "Now, you take those folks. You don't know if they're comin' or goin.' They could have busted and are movin' onto another dream. Or, maybe, they're takin' the fruits of their labor to market from this dream. What did you used to dream about?" I asked him.

"I always wanted to be a major chief in the Chickasaw Nation. I wanted to be respected and honored and lead my people to a better life in the time-honored ways of the Chickasaws. I wanted to be the greatest hunter, the fastest runner, the best tracker. All the things a young Indian wants to prove to himself and others. And you?"

"I gave up dreamin' for opportunity. My daddy didn't believe in dreamin.' He'd knock me in the head if he thought I had my head in the clouds. I took the opportunity to leave at the earliest possible convenience."

"And, here we sit. One of us a purveyor of liquid fire and the other a consumer. We're both at the effect of a pernicious liquid that has little value except for the enjoyment it brings inside the stomach of the imbiber."

"Where did you get all those four-bit words? I can't follow half of what you said. What was that, a surveyor? Pernicious? Wasn't he a Greek soldier in the Trojan War?

"A purveyor is a distributor and pernicious is causing great harm and ruinous. As for the Trojan War, I didn't know any

Creek Indians fought that far away from home."

"By golly, I think I could get to like you after a bit. Let me bring you a bottle of sarsaparilla. You look like you could use a good drink."

"Sarsaparilla? Are you trying to poison me? I thought you liked me?"

"Don't complain until you try it. Besides, I've got lots of bottles in there with labels that don't always match the contents," I said. "You know I can't sell alcohol to an Indian. Especially with a U.S. marshal watchin' us."

"Where?"

"Down under that cottonwood over there. You're slippin."

"I've been around white men too long."

"I can appreciate that one." I came back out with several bottles and handed one to George. As soon as I did, the marshal came trotting his horse over to us.

"I finally caught you, D.W."

"Oh, Marshal Swain, get down off your horse and join us. Have a bottle of sarsaparilla."

"I know you better than that. Give me that bottle Big Tree."

George hadn't taken a sip from the bottle and handed it up to Swain. The marshal took a big swig out of the bottle. He spit the sweet tasting liquid all over the side of the saloon. "Damn, that's sarsaparilla. That stuff is terrible."

"I told you marshal. You know I wouldn't break any laws like that."

"Damn you, Sweden. We found your still again. Broke it into little pieces."

"My still?" I asked. "Where would you get an idea like that? If my wife thought I had a still, she'd never let me hear the end of it."

"Well, you haven't heard the end of it. We'll catch you soon enough."

"I don't doubt it. You want to take the rest of the sarsaparilla with you? I'll need to charge you for the bottle."

He screwed up his face in a disgusted look and threw the bottle down on the sand. "That sweet tooth you Indians have will be the death of you yet," he said as he rode away.

"How did you know he was down there?" George asked. "I may be getting old but my eyesight isn't that bad."

"I just guessed. Whenever he's in town he always follows the Indians across the river. Used to catch the guy who had your old Indian blanket all the time. I figured he couldn't miss that red and white flag you had on. Here, have a real sarsaparilla. Make sure you keep it up to your lips like you're takin' a long sip."

"Hmmm. Great sarsaparilla. I thought you didn't sell to the Indians."

"I don't. I always leave a few jars sittin' around the still and they suddenly appear across the river. Then one mornin' I find a jar with a few dollars in it sittin' on the porch. I always figured it was the whiskey fairy leavin' me some extra money."

"I haven't seen your still of late over in the nation."

"I moved it over to Oklahoma Territory so they couldn't get me for haulin' whiskey through Indian Territory."

"The marshal told you he tore up your still. What will you do now?"

"I'll wait a week or two and then go see if it was my still or someone else's. If it was mine, then I'll move it to another spot and try again. They'll get tired of watchin' the spot after a week or so."

"You keep making money on the thirst of some poor savage who has no control over his desire for liquor. That would seem a sorry way to make a living."

"No. A sorry way of makin' a livin' is by trying to grow crops in solid rock. If rocks and stones were a cash crop I wouldn't have gotten into the whiskey business. Besides, this won't last very long. It's gettin' too civilized. I can't find a place to hide the still anymore where nobody would discover it. The marshal gives a reward for turnin' in stills and moonshiners. It ain't much, but for some of these dirt grubbers, it's the only money they'll see this year. It's harder to keep from gettin' caught. It won't be worth it much longer."

"You have no idea," George said. "There is a move afoot in Washington to create a single state from the two territories. No more Cherokee Nation. No more Creek Nation. No more Seminole Nation. No more Choctaw Nation." Then, very quietly, "No more Chickasaw Nation."

George sighed and stared at his bottle. "And no more whiskey."

"What?"

"That's right. The way things are going now, the new state will be dry. The prohibitionists are winning that battle. They are going to save the noble red man from himself. And, these saloons will be a long gone memory, blowing away in the wind. Just like the promises the white man made us."

"A dry state. I'm goin' to have to write to somebody about this. Oh, hell, I'll just pack up and leave for Colorado."

"What good will that do?"

"Won't do any good at all, but it will get me away from these fools who keep tryin' to save me. Not a single one of them ever asked me if I wanted to be saved. No. They just come in and change things that don't need changin.'"

"You would have made a good Indian."

"Can I use you as a reference? I can use the help in gettin' a land allotment. That's the way this is going to go."

He laughed. "The only way you can get a land allotment is if you can fool the tribal council. With that pale white skin and that bushy mustache, I doubt seriously you could even fool the Indian agent. And those people are easy to fool."

"Well, it doesn't hurt to try. What's one more scam? At least the family will have some place to stay."

"You're serious. You've been drinking way too much of your own beverage."

"Actually, I prefer sarsaparilla. My stomach can't take the alcohol. Burns a hole in my gut if I take more than a taste. I've got to find a way to feed the family when this goes away," I said waving at the saloon.

"Now who sounds maudlin?"

"This old river has washed away a lot of dreams and a lot of bad memories. The last time it washed away the saloon and a good friend of mine, I knew that it wouldn't be here for eternity. It's like watchin' a prairie fire racin' towards your barn full of hay. Your whole year is going to be wiped out and there's not a thing you can do about it but watch. It's in that moment when you know your whole future is goin' up in flames that you stop and plan for something else. I've seen the fire and I've seen the flood and I've already started plannin' for the time when the next one comes."

"You always have a charming turn of phrase. Perhaps there's hope for you white people yet. But, I doubt it," George said. "Some of the most eloquent speakers in this land have been Indians who have a deep love of the land and a passion for living without restraints. Yet you do not listen. And, you keep finding ways to restrict the freedom of those around you. Living in your little brown and white boxes and pretending you know about the natural order of things. I think your buildings with wooden floors allow you to be close yet keep you so far away from Mother Earth. That is why you do not listen."

"We don't listen because we already know better. We don't have anything to learn from the Indians. We have things to teach you."

"Like how to make whiskey. How to spread disease. How to take what isn't yours. How to scar the landscape and kill the animals. You know, I never saw anyone kill an animal for the sake of killing until the white man came. Then, everything became a target. Shoot an animal for the size of its horns? What insanity," George raved.

"You can't be that far gone on a single bottle of sarsaparilla. You should give that stuff up and drink soda water."

"If you had any good whiskey, I would mix soda water with

it. However, I'll settle for this odd-tasting concoction. You're right. I do get wound up about what I see happening here. Trouble is I can't run away to Colorado. They'd just send me back. You can't get away from the white man anymore. There are no more open plains or free-roaming buffalo herds or deer. All you see are those cursed wagons with their high-topped white canvas. Cities and towns and fences. More gifts from the white man."

"You know, George, maybe you've stayed in Washington too long. Maybe a few months out here with the coyotes and dust storms will clear your head."

"I'll drink to that. Where do I find that whiskey fairy of yours? I'm obviously going to have to make new arrangements for my continued connection to the spirits."

"He'll contact you. That way you won't have to worry about runnin' into him. Besides, I can always bring you some sarsaparilla up to Red Hill."

George got up and headed for the walkway. As he left he said, "At least that's one thing that won't change. That red clay hill will still be standing long after we're gone."

"The sand bar saloon and the gambling tent attachment is becoming quite a stench in the nostrils of the people of this community. A number of robberies are said to have been recently committed there. While we have no sympathy for the man who is robbed in such places, being of the opinion that he is but paying a just penalty for being at such a place, there is no question but what he is entitled to full protection from the law and the officers should see that this place is broken up."

. . . The Purcell Register, Dec. 4, 1891

Chapter 18

There was one thing about owning a saloon in the Twin Territories that was always bothersome. These places were like magnets for every thief and would-be robber from Dallas to Wichita and from Ft. Smith to Amarillo. Purcell was one of those places that never had a problem with train robbers. Because the depot was between the bluff and the river, there was no way to beat an easy retreat. That didn't stop any of the hardcases from sitting on the front porch of the Floating Palace and making plans to be the first.

Along the owlhoot trail, you were known more by the company you kept than by anything you might have done. There were horse thieves and cattle rustlers and armed robbers out to make a reputation. The Twin Territories were the breeding and stomping grounds for some of the worst desperadoes in the West. The Younger brothers lived there before they ended up in prison after the Northfield, Minnesota, raid in '76. The Daltons were relatives of the Youngers and came to a much more permanent end in Coffeyville, Kansas, in '92.

After that, the Bill Dalton-Bill Doolin gang was the scourge of the territories. By this time, they didn't have to cart you all the way to Ft. Smith for a trial. Every street corner had a U.S. deputy marshal on it. Thankfully, for small fish like us, the really big guns chased after the Dalton-Doolin gang and left us on our own.

The Floating Palace Saloon was pretty lucky when it came to being left alone. I mentioned you were known by the company you kept. Well, it just so happens that our old poker-playing buddies were now part of that gang. Bitter Creek Newcombe, Charlie Pierce and Tulsa Jack Blake had joined in with the Daltons a time or two but had known Bill Doolin a lot longer. With the Dalton gang out of the way, their new gang was known as the Oklahombres.

I made a special effort to point out the names carved in the bar. Bitter Creek, Charlie and Tulsa Jack were immortalized in pine board. Of course, I was always sure to mention the story about the three yahoos we dragged out of the saloon. For some reason, I never did point out that the boys didn't stay long enough to help us carry the carcasses out let alone carve something in the bar.

Just the mention of the names was enough to put the fear of god-knows-what in the two-bit blowhards that came by the saloon. That and the solid deck and walls around us kept most of the trouble outside where we liked it.

On a cold, windy December day, the door blew open and in came two men wearing windbreakers and carrying shotguns. It was too early in the day for us to have much money in the till and it was too bright for an easy getaway.

"You the owner of this place?" the one in front said. He was kind of dumpy looking in a brown suit with a watch chain hanging from his vest pocket.

"I'm one of them," I replied. "D.W. Sweden. What can I get you?"

"Here it is Chris," the second one said, pointing to the names carved in the bar.

The second one turned back to me. "My name's Chris Madsen. I'm a deputy U.S. marshal assigned to run down the Doolin-Dalton gang. We understand you know the gang real well."

"Well, marshal, I wouldn't say that. I've played poker with them a couple of times back some time ago."

"That's not what I heard. I understand that this place is under their protection. My deputy says you paid them to kill some toughs here," he said.

"Say, you've got a funny accent. I've heard that before up in Michigan. Let's see, Scandinavian isn't it?"

I could see him biting his lip, making his bushy mustache do a funny dance across the bottom half of his face. He looked at his deputy. "How long would it take to close this place?"

"Oh, about two minutes."

"You've got two minutes to tell me what I want to hear," he said with a grim smile. "And, don't try to change the subject again."

"Okay. If you promise not to let anybody know, I'll tell you. This is just between you, me and the fence post."

He glared at me. "Go ahead."

"I'm sure you know about the reputation that Sand Bar Town has. There are guys that come through here that would just as soon shoot you as look at you. I myself am a peaceable man. The only gun I've got is an old scatter-gun kind of like the ones you're carrying. I only use it if someone tries to rob us or rough up the house. Since I carved those nicknames in the bar and spread around that story, no one has bothered us while a few other places have been shot up pretty good."

"When was the last time you saw them?"

"Oh, it's been about a year ago."

"How can you be so sure? Something smells fishy about this," Madsen said.

"It was a little while after Black-Face Charley Bryant shot it out with that deputy marshal."

"Right."

"No. Really. The first time I met them was about two years ago. It was Tulsa Jack, Bitter Creek, Charlie Pierce and Black-Face Charley. They talked about wantin' to put some excitement in their lives. I tried to talk 'em out of it, but they were hell bent for leather. Then, they came through again last year. This time, it was without Bryant. They played poker for awhile and took a couple of railroad big shots for a bundle. Some guys came in and tried to hold up the poker game and the boys talked them out of it. Of course, they let their six-shooters do the talking. I played it up a bit so's we wouldn't be bothered."

Madsen started laughing. I never did understand why I had that effect on so many people. He wiped the tears out of his eyes. "I've heard some strange stories since I've been here, but yours stretches the bounds of credibility."

"But, it's the truth."

"Unfortunately, I believe you. No one could make something like that up. When's the last time you saw Dalton or Doolin?"

"Never have seen them. They talked about Doolin. Used to work with him on the ranches up along the Cimarron. As far as I know, he's never stopped by here. They talked about the Dalton brothers, but not Bill Dalton. After their fiasco in Coffeyville, you'd think those boys would know better," I went on.

"The only thing that will stop them is a bullet," he said in an off-handed manner. He walked to the back and looked around the store room. Then, he went to the end of the bar and looked at the carvings. He shook his head. "Crazy saloon owners."

He walked to the front window and looked across at the railway station. "You can see Purcell very well from here. Why do you have to walk over those steps to get into the saloon?"

"It's a boat."

He laughed again.

"No, really. It's built like a barge. The one drawback to being in the middle of the river is that it floods down here a lot. Just last June this thing was swept downriver. We had to dig it out of the sand and float it back up the river. Otherwise, we'd be out of business."

"I'm going to leave you in business," he paused, "for awhile. The only thing that will keep you from a worse fate than the river is to let my deputies know the minute that one of the Dalton-Doolin gang walks in the door. If I hear, even a peep, about outlaws using this place for a resting spot and I'll personally come burn the place down. Then, you won't have to worry about the river," he smiled. "Do I make myself clear?"

"Crystal," I replied.

He walked out shaking his head, muttering, "A boat with a saloon. Some fool with a penknife carves outlaw names in his bar." He turned back to me for a second, "Are you crazy?"

I took it that he really didn't want an answer since he didn't stay around long enough to hear my reply. Robert and Sandy sauntered in the back door about the time Madsen was going out the front.

"I see somebody else has met you for the first time," she said. "Who was that?"

"Some guy lookin' for the Dalton-Doolin gang."

Robert snorted, "Try that one again."

"A deputy marshal, name of Chris Madsen. He heard about our guardian angels there on the end of the bar and wanted an explanation."

Sandy snickered. "He came to the right man. I don't think I could have kept a straight face telling that story."

"Well, you've got that right for a change. Of course, he couldn't keep a straight face while I told it."

"How come he didn't haul you off to jail?"

"Nothin' around here to get us for. We're runnin' one of the cleanest businesses in the valley."

"What are you talking about?" Sandy kept on her harangue. "You're one of the biggest moonshiners in the territory."

"The only way they can prove that is to catch me at the still. I've got one hell of a flock of chickens in that hollow. Anyone sets a foot anywhere near me, those chickens set up a cackling that a deaf person could hear. By the time anyone gets close to the still, I've hightailed it to high ground. Anything I bring in here is in a bottle and looks official. We don't sell liquor to the Indians anywhere near the saloon. Besides, those guys are lookin' for one thing and one thing only and that's the Dalton-Doolin gang."

"Madsen, Madsen, that name sounds familiar."

"Should be, he's one of the three big guns they've sent after the gang. Him and Bill Tilghman and Heck Thomas are called the Three Guardsmen."

"Damn, this place is getting too much attention from the law," Robert complained.

"Now, there's attention and there's attention," I said.

"Does this mean we're about to get doused with some more rural wisdom?" Sandy asked. "If so, I can go upstairs and get ready for this evening's business."

"Maybe you should go ahead upstairs anyway. It'll take you about this long to get in any kind of shape to attract customers," I sniped at her.

"Robert," she shrilled. "Take your gun out and shoot this mad dog. He has insulted me for the last time."

"Wait just a minute," I retorted, "I don't get upset over your little insults about the saloon and how you fancied up the second story.

"You sure must be crazy to be attracted to somebody like that," I told Robert.

"You just can't find women with spirit anymore. She's got a fire in her soul that lights up my life."

"Well, she's got a fire in her soul that gives me heartburn," I said. "As I was saying before I was so rudely interrupted, you can tell the difference between a lawman on the prod and a lawman lookin' for an advantage. These guys know that they can shut me down but that the saloon would be open again tomorrow. We're much more valuable to them if we can supply them with information. If that doesn't cost them anymore than a threat, then they got off cheaply."

"I don't think I'll ever understand you, D.W. I've been in saloons from New Orleans to Denver and you've got the strangest attitude I've ever known."

"Hey, I paid attention to the saloonkeepers in those cow towns in Kansas. They kept gettin' rowdier and rowdier until the townfolks finally got up the guts to shut 'em down. That's something I'm tryin' to avoid. We can't fight off the robbers and the citizens. Them judges is kind of nasty when it comes to gunplay and such."

"Why did they believe you, then?"

"Didn't somebody ever tell you that truth makes a better story? These guys are used to listenin' to tall tales. The truth overwhelms 'em because they aren't used to it from guys like us. You asked me why I was different. It's because I read the paper a lot and I watch people and I listen. You usually don't get in trouble unless your mouth is runnin' off faster than your brain is," I told him.

"Yeah, but you don't look like someone who can read."

"My granddaddy tried to grow crops in the rocks of upstate New York. My dad moved to Ohio where there was a little more dirt than rocks, but it was still hard work. Me and Linc were born in Ohio and then dad moved on into Michigan. He finally found that farmland he was lookin' for. Linc and I moved on because there were too many boys in the family and the place wasn't big enough for all of us. For some reason, granddad pushed readin' and writin.' He said that no man could make anything of himself without readin' or writin.' Mom was a midwife and she wanted to be able to read and write so she could put down the birthdates and stuff for people in their family Bibles. I just like to read. Don't believe much of what's in the paper, but it's a good way to pass the time of day."

"Sandy and I have been talking about moving on," he said, changing the subject rather abruptly.

"You don't mean that little summer rainstorm is botherin' her?"

"It's more than that. The customers are a lot rougher and it's harder for her to keep girls. She won't come near the place if there's even a thunderhead in the sky. She's like me, she can't see rebuilding this place if it gets torn apart again."

"You know better than to leave in the middle of a run of good luck," I said. "We were up and runnin' before anyone else was even close to bein' open. We made more money in that month than any other time since we've been in business. What more could you want?"

"A royal flush in five-card stud. I'm getting maudlin in my old age. Most of the lawmen I knew were bigger thieves than the ones they were chasing. Now, I see these damned sober marshals coming through here and it makes me nervous. I must admit, though, this is the first time I've owned my own place and I kind of like it."

"You just keep ridin' the streak till it runs out. I won't say this is the mother lode, but it sure beats the hell out of workin' for a livin.' It's the first time in a long time that I can remember my wife not givin' me grief about what I was or wasn't doin.' That makes it worthwhile for me for sure. I love my wife but sometimes that voice of hers is shrill enough to strip the hairs off a dog's back. I'm happy when she settles down and tones it down."

"What about those guys?" he asked, pointing towards the end of the bar.

I smiled. "Lady luck brought them in and out of the saloon before they had built up their reputations. These law dogs will be on their trails till they're buried. They can't afford to come to a place like this. Too much traffic and too many people lookin' to collect the rewards on them. No, we won't see them again. That marshal's threat was useless. I'll make up a story and these dregs of humanity will avoid us even more."

Sandy had come back downstairs. "We can't keep the dregs away. He keeps showing up behind the bar," she added, pointing her thumb at me.

"Don't you have someone else you could go haunt? Maybe someone needs a scarecrow to keep his corn patch safe. That way, your mouth and your bloomers could be flappin' in the wind somewhere useful," I said.

"Robert, shoot him. No jury would convict you. It would be self-defense. I'd testify in your favor at the coroner's inquest. There aren't any other witnesses. Please. Do it for me. Do it for the community. Oh, hell, just do it."

Robert smiled his quirky little smile and I stood there wondering if the bar and the gambling could support us.

"Maybe I ought to tell those marshals that the only reason the Oklahombres come by is to see you. They could put you in protective custody and hope they come to spring you. By the time that happens, hell will be frozen over and I will have moved on."

"You wouldn't dare," she snarled.

"Yeah," Robert said, with hesitation, "you wouldn't do that."

"Peace and quiet. I like peace and quiet. I'd settle for that, wouldn't you?"

"The cooks at the Vienna Cafe and Weitzenhoffer's restaurant got into a scrap one afternoon this week and tried to make hash of each other. Both were considerably stove up in the contest."
                        . . . The Purcell Register, Aug. 28, 1891

Chapter 19

For some of the folks that made the land run in `89, there wasn't much to laugh about. A lot of them were accused of being claim jumpers and others would never make it as farmers. In the midst of all this boom and bust, a man had to keep his sense of humor. I may not have agreed with everything that was ever written in The Purcell Register, but I must admit they did have a sense of humor.

There was the time when some fellow named Frank Gowan and two cohorts took a skiff out on the river late one afternoon. They were singing "Life on the Ocean Wave" as they floated downstream. Not much sillier than folks in a rowboat in the middle of summer pretending they were on an ocean voyage. What was really strange, though, was the number of people who came down to watch them off.

A few of the sporting types around town think of themselves as masterful hunters. However, when Jim Holyfield, P.S. Eskridge, P.M. DeVitt and S.A. McMurray went out one Saturday, they shot 76 rounds but managed to hit only one quail and one rabbit. These boys were pretty good sports though because they could tell one on themselves. They even admitted that the dog caught the rabbit. The paper took a potshot at them and was much closer to the mark. "Say, Jim, the next time you scare up a flock of quails, don't cock the right hand barrel of your gun and pull the left hand trigger."

One story I remember is about an Alaskan Indian that was sentenced to ninety-nine years in prison for murder. He asked the judge if the government was going to keep him alive long enough to serve the sentence or would they let him out when he died. That's my kind of logic.

A couple of years ago, a passel of robbers came through Purcell, looking for some loot. They were obviously a bunch of amateur robbers, but professional bunglers. They tried to break into the safe at R.G. Hall & Son's store. They drilled the safe for what must have been a long time, but came up a half-inch short in their efforts. Somebody said their drill bit wasn't long enough. They apparently didn't bother looking through the store for a longer bit. They grabbed some dry goods and took off. One of the other merchants took advantage of the event to make this announcement: "Mr. J.L. Berringer says the robbers broke into his hardware store and found his goods all marked so low that it wouldn't pay to steal them."

That sense of humor helps in any business, especially for a saloonkeeper. Charley Lissauer lost his sense of humor after that storm washed away his bar. Sam had finally talked him out of having a saloon in the middle of the river. From then on, he sat on a bench out in front of Little Sam's Saloon and talked about all his dreams for the fortune he should have made.

Tom and Ray Farmer had rebuilt the Ark. One day, Tom came running through the front door like his tail was on fire.

"Slow down before you hurt yourself," I told him.

"I need you in court tomorrow or the next day," he said rather brusquely. "It's damned important that you be there. We need you to testify."

"Do I look like a singin' canary to you?" Don't you know you can catch your death of cold from a bad draft in the courthouse? You can go in the front door and never come out again. I know. I'm still waitin' for some of my friends to come back."

"What in the hell are you bellowing about?"

"I don't go to court unless someone with a gun and a badge decides to escort me," I said.

"That can be arranged. This ain't that big a deal even for you. All you have to do is identify a keg of whiskey."

"Do I have to pick it out of a crowd? Is it armed and

dangerous?"

"Will you knock off the horse crap?"

"Now wait a minute," I said. "You're the one who came bargin` in here wantin' me to go to court to identify some whiskey keg and you've got the nerve to tell me I should knock off the crap. In a pig's eye."

"I'm serious."

"Bein' serious and bein' sane are two different things and I think you're more of the first and less of the second."

"All right. Do you remember that rise in the river we had a couple of weeks ago? The one that knocked our saloon off its posts."

"Sure," I said. "It was funny watching you sittin' up on the corner of the roof. The water wasn't that deep."

"The hell you say. If you can't swim, any depth is too deep. Anyway, that's where our problem started. Some of our whiskey kegs were swept down river by the current. We found out some sod-buster name of H.H. Clarke found one of the kegs and took it home with him. When we found out about it, we went to get it. He wouldn't let anyone near his house. He's been sampling the contents because he and some of his friends have been drinking and bragging about it. We're trying to get the keg and what's left back. He keeps saying `finders keepers' and that is annoying," Tom finally explained.

"One keg of whiskey looks just like any other keg," I told him. "What makes you think I can help you?"

"Because it's one of your kegs. And, I know you keep track of those."

"But someone might get the idea that I make liquor or something to that effect and that could be detrimental to my freedom," I argued.

"Look, we filed a replevin suit against this farmer in Justice of the Peace Gwynn's court. You don't have to go into any great detail about why you know that keg belongs to us. We just need somebody from another establishment to testify for us. I know you can make up a story that will explain why you know that keg. I've heard some of your stories."

"Now, you want me to go commit perjury. This damned keg better be lined with gold or silver."

"Just be there. We don't ask you for much, but this one should be relatively easy. We've got a bottle of bonded bourbon that you can have if you'll do this."

"Does it have the tax stamp on it?"

"You bet."

"All right, I'll be there."

The next morning saw me down at the justice of the peace staring around at the huge crowd that had gathered to hear the whiskey keg case. A replevin suit, I found out, was an action to recover personal property unlawfully taken. I swear there were more people here for this piddling suit than any of the murders we'd had over the last year. Even some of the finer ladies of town were sitting in on this one.

The justice of the peace did all the questioning. He started with Clarke. After sparring with the justice for a few minutes, Clarke finally admitted he didn't own the keg and that other than finding it, he had no claim on it.

"So, I don't see any other course except to turn the keg back over to Mr. Farmer," the justice said.

"But, your honor," Clarke said. "It took a lot of hard work to recover that keg. There's a lot of skill involved in getting around that quicksand in the riverbottom. I dare say neither one of them would have been able to recover the keg if they found it. They should have at least offered me a finder's fee."

I was in the back row breathing a deep sigh of relief since I didn't have to testify. Tom stood up and agreed with the justice to pay a $10 reward for return of the keg. The gavel came down and the case was closed. The crowd went away disappointed that more fireworks didn't result from the shenanigans in court.

I caught up with Tom at the top of Depot Hill. "When can I come get my bottle of bonded?"

"What bottle?"

"The one you promised for testifyin.'"

"You know I don't carry that kind of whiskey. I just made that up so you'd go. Besides, you didn't even testify," he said.

"Sounds to me like you're crawfishin' out of our deal. Maybe I'll file some kind of breach of contract suit against you."

"Go ahead," he laughed. "I'd love to see you being questioned by some judge or justice."

"I had a feelin' this wasn't goin' to work out," I said. "Next time you're sittin' on the top of your saloon in a flood, I'm goin' to leave you there."

Nothing worse than being taken by some damned Farmer, I thought. Maybe I should have helped that other farmer with a keg up.

By the time I got back to the saloon, my favorite snake oil salesman had camped out at the end of the bar and was waiting for me. The only reason Honest John Barnes was my favorite is that he liked to mix my liquor into his snake oil and he paid well for it. Of course, that's how you learned that the honest part of his name had nothing to do with the way he did business.

"Why if it ain't ol' Honest John himself," I greeted him. "I just got cheated out of a bottle of bonded bourbon by the guy next door. What is it you want to do for me?"

"I'm always glad to see you too, D.W. How's the worst moonshiner in the territories doing today?"

"I have no idea. You'll have to go ask him if they'll let you in the jail. What am I saying? Of all people, of course they'd let you in the jail. They'd even give you a long-term lease agreement at their expense."

Skunkbit was in the saloon for one of his early rounds. He looked at the two of us as though he expected us to come to blows. "I thought you liked each other. It don't sound that way to me."

I just laughed. "Don't worry about it none. John and I have been tradin' barbs at each other for quite a few years now. He's used to it and I don't pay him no mind. Besides, if you're a whiskey peddler, whether it's from a wagon or behind the bar, you have a kind of kinship. Everything I say to him, pretty much, applies to me, too. Anyway, he hasn't come up with an original insult in nigh onto two years. I think he's slippin' or maybe it's sippin' too much of his product."

John laughed as well. "D.W. taught me every trick of the trade from the fancy labels on the bottles to how to cover the taste of the whiskey. Trouble with him is that he's been rooted in one place too long. He's started to grow mold. I would say he's starting to smell funny but he's always smelled funny."

I picked up a bottle that was sitting in front of Skunkbit. "What's this stuff?"

"D.W., that little product will sell thousands and thousands of bottles. You have no idea how popular that stuff is. As a matter of fact, I need some more of your rootstock for my tonic."

"Dr. Scalpel's Canadian Country Cure, the cutting edge of medicinal healing. Any disease cured. Any body organ healed. Ideal for colds, consumption, coughs, rheumatism, arthritis, headaches, fevers, blood diseases, chills, biliousness and others," I read.

Skunkbit pointed to the bottle and said, "Yeah, I had a drink of that and already I feel better."

"I didn't know you were sick," I replied.

"Neither did I, but old Honest John here pointed out that I could still have blood poison from that rabies. Not enough to kill me, but just enough to make me feel a little peaked. I haven't been feeling right for the last couple of days. I'll have to buy me a bottle," he said.

"The only thing wrong with you is that you started to sober up and that had you feelin' a little off your feed," I told him. Turning to John, "Honest, John, I don't know how you do it. I swear you could sell cow dung to a farmer and convince him it was like no fertilizer he'd ever seen."

"Now that you mention it, I did that once. But it wasn't

cow dung, it was elephant dung. Great stuff. Makes crops grow to the size of elephants."

I threw a towel at him. "That will probably make somebody a great song some day. You're cuttin' into my business sellin' that stuff in here."

John waved at Skunkbit. "The bottle's yours. My friend and I have some business to do."

He grabbed my arm and headed for the table closest to the back wall. He lowered his voice so only I could hear him. "I tell you I found the mother lode. This stuff tastes so bad it makes them feel good once they get it down and let its soothing effects course through their bodies. I found a way to cover the taste of your liquor so's they can't tell what it is that makes them feel so good. I even sold some to a preacher lady. She hasn't been the same since."

"Who was that?"

"Let me see," he mused, "oh, yeah, a Fountains. Beverly Fountains."

I started laughing so hard I couldn't keep my seat. I sprawled on the floor, banging my head on the chair. He jumped up and pulled me upright and sat me back in the chair.

"What's wrong with you? People see you like this and they'll think something is wrong with my medicine."

"That's ol' Preacher Ben Fountain's wife. She's been tryin' to close down Sand Bar Town since her husband was hit by lightnin'" across the river here. Now you got her hooked on my booze. That is somethin' I couldn't even dream up."

"Look. I've got to have a wagon load of your finest within a week. I've got a contract with a company that will bottle it and put it on the market for me. We can be rich."

"Are you crazy? If I try to run my still solid for the amount of time it would take to make that much liquor, they'd catch me for sure. Then, you'd be visitin' me in the hoosegow."

"I'll make it worth your while. Double what I usually pay you. I am desperate. Yours is the only moonshine I can find that gives my medicine its unique taste. I've got to have it."

"What have you been mixin' in my liquor to make it taste like medicine?"

"Blackberries."

"Blackberries. Yecch! I can't even imagine how that would taste."

"With everybody else's moonshine, it tastes like blackberry brandy and smells like wood alcohol. With yours, it tastes like a sweet batch of castor oil and smells like liniment. I have farmers' wives and shopkeepers and mothers and grandmothers coming from all over the territory trying to get their hands on this stuff. You know you can't sit back and wait when something like this happens. Strike while the iron is hot. Dig when the ground ain't frozen. Pluck when the fruit is ripe."

"All right. All right. I have a feelin' the only pluckin' that's goin' to be done is from my hide. Is this goin' to happen a lot or is this just a one time deal?"

"If this batch sells as well as the first batch, then it could be for a long time."

"Make it two-and-a-half times as much and you got a deal. If the marshals get too close, though, you won't be able to track me with a pack of bloodhounds. If they're breathing down my neck, the deal's off."

"You never worried much about them before."

"Me and ol' L.G. Swilling out there have been doin' this for years at a slow pace with limited run times. You can smell that mash for a long way off and there's too many settlers around here nowadays to get away with it like I used to."

"Who is this damned L.G. Swilling? I've heard that name for a long time. You told me he's one of the biggest whiskey runners in the territory. You always told me he was the one that made the whiskey. As far as I know, nobody's ever caught him."

"L.G. is the fastest moonshiner on four feet."

"Huh?"

"If you promise not to tell anybody else, I'll point him out.

Otherwise, I'll have to keep it a secret. Liquid Gold and I have been brayin' about our activities for years but nobody was really listenin'"

"Liquid Gold?"

"You sound more confused now than when we started this conversation. You got to promise to keep this to yourself. It's the only way you'll get anymore moonshine out of me."

"Okay. I'll keep it under my hat."

"Liquid Gold Swilling is my mule. You know, L.G. for short."

"Your m. . . "

I got my hand over his face before he had a chance to mention the mule. This was getting to be a habit. I decided then and there to keep things to myself.

"Are you crazy?"

I laughed. "You know I am. If the marshals are out lookin' for an L.G. Swilling, they won't come lookin' for me. In the early days, I sold all my liquor through L.G. I'd tell people he made it and I sold it. Since I opened this saloon, most of my sales have been out the back door once the liquor is in a proper keg or bottle. As far as bein' the biggest whiskey runner in the territory, he stands seventeen hands high. I can turn him loose and he'll find his way back here without a problem. That's one smart mule."

He groaned. "And here I thought all this time I was just dealing with some mule-headed moonshiner."

"See," I said. "All these years you were right."

Finally, he started laughing. "What has kept you out of jail?"

"Well, a mule, a few chickens and a lot of luck. That's why I have to be careful this time around. Civilization does something to your luck. I don't know what. But, I'm just not takin' the chances I used to take."

"But, for me you'll do it."

"For you and a few gold coins, I can be talked into just about anything."

"What's put the fear of God in you?"

"Mother Nature. That old woman is as contrary as any female I ever met. She's warm and sweet one minute and a cold, ravin' witch the next. We've lost the saloon once to a flood and almost lost it twice. I can't afford that second loss. If it goes this time, I have to have some money in the pot."

"Why should that bother you? You'd just find some other scam to get after."

"This bar has been good to me. I am plain tired of not havin' a pot to pee in nor a window to throw it out of. My wife is puttin' the money into a farm over west of Purcell. She's happy. I'm happy. But, Mother Nature is a certified tail twister. She'll crawl out from under that back porch and bite you in the ass when you least expect it."

"Hmmm. I'll have your money at the end of next week."

"I should have your whiskey."

"You're not giving me much encouragement."

"Didn't I ever tell you that you need to develop a sense of humor about this stuff? If you don't get your whiskey, laugh. It'll only hurt for a little while."

"If I don't get that tonic, it'll hurt for a hell of a lot longer than that."

I shook my head. "Don't worry none. Besides if Dr. Scalpel's cure don't kill 'em, then the disease surely won't."

"The vigilant constabulary of the Territory sometimes displays great energy in arresting a party for a little game of high five, but a gambling den can run wide open on Main street without molestation."

... *The Purcell Register, Jan. 29, 1892*

Chapter 20

September 1893 was the kind of month that folks who write histories like to tell stories about. In a single month, the Twin Territories showed the worst and the best of approaching statehood. At one end of the territory, civilization came in with another land rush. While the other end of the territory, an event occurred that showed just how far away civilization really was.

The biggest land rush ever held went off on Sept. 16 in the Cherokee Outlet. Somewhere over 100,000 people put on a mad rush for 50,000 claims in the strip. Half the population of Purcell and Lexington were gone for this land rush. The first part of September was real quiet in our part of the territory because all the gamblers and con men had headed for the Outlet to take advantage of a whole new set of erstwhile homesteaders.

With all our best customers off chasing some tomfool land grab, business was the worst. And, the month started off on the wrong foot for the Floating Palace Saloon because of the uncivilized event.

On Sept. 2, Robert and I were moving tables, trying to get a new gaming wheel into the room. The door burst open and a highly agitated Deputy Marshal Swain came in the front door.

"Have you seen any of the Dalton-Doolin Gang today?"

"Not on your life. If they'd come through that door, I'd have let you know in no time at all."

"They're in the territory looking for a place to hole up," the marshal said, his face red. "I'm going to put a couple of deputies upstairs to watch for them."

"Really. We haven't seen them for a long time," Robert

added. "We don't need their kind of trouble."

"You ain't seen trouble yet."

"What happened?" Robert asked.

"You ain't heard? Them bastards shot up some deputy marshals in Ingalls yesterday. Killed three of them and got clean away. We think they shot Newcomb and Dalton, but the rest cleared the town and headed for ground."

"Ingalls? Where's that? I haven't heard of that place," I told him.

"Its over east of Stillwater in Payne County. Damned outlaws have been usin' it as a waterin' hole for a long time."

"See," I told the marshal, "they found another place to frequent. We're a long ways from their home range."

"Yeah, but they'll be looking for a friendly place to go and this is a likely spot for them to try since it is away from their usual haunts," Swain noted.

"Why don't you just track them down instead of roustin' us?" I asked. "Something like that happens, I'd think you'd have every marshal in the territory on their trail."

"If it was up to me, we would run them to ground and nail their hides to the closest tree. But, that damned land run is coming up in a couple of weeks and every spare marshal is up along the boundary somewhere trying to keep those sodbusters from crossing the line early. It's a hell of a note. Damned politicians are ruining the territory," he said.

"Who are you lookin' for? Maybe we can spot 'em faster if we know who they are."

"Bill Doolin, Bill Dalton, Tulsa Jack Blake, Bitter Creek Newcomb, Charlie Pierce, Dynamite Dick Clifton. We'll get every blasted one of them for this," he said, bitterly.

"Those boys should have known when to quit," I said.

"If I've said it once, I've said it a thousand times, they'll quit when somebody shoots them," the marshal added. He headed for the front door. "A deputy will be by later tonight. Put him in the front room upstairs."

After he left, I looked at Robert, "You get to tell Sandy she's a room short tonight."

Robert looked at me disgustedly, "Won't make any difference. Once everybody learns there's a deputy on the premises, they won't come within a mile of the place. I guarantee we won't have any customers."

"You're probably right about that," I said.

Sandy came sauntering in the back door with her arms full of packages. She was smiling and her face was slightly flushed. "My new wardrobe came in today. I can't wait to try these on."

Robert smiled. "Go ahead. I'd love to see you in a new outfit."

"Anything to improve the view," I mumbled.

"Robert. If you don't shoot him this time, I will. My new derringer came in with the order."

She left to go upstairs and I watched her go. "She sure ain't the same woman we pulled off'n that stage."

"No, she isn't. I'm a changed man, too. I think you were right earlier when you told the marshal that those boys should have known when to quit. I don't know about you, but I think it's time that Sandy and I quit this saloon and moved on."

"Where to?"

"I don't know. Denver. San Francisco. Maybe even Los Angeles. Somewhere we can start over and nobody knows us."

"Well, hell, you could move to Tulsa and change your name and nobody would know you," I told him.

"Not quite the same, D.W. You know, this is the first time in my life that I've stayed at any one place more than a few months. The way some of those folks in Purcell look down on me, you'd think I had the plague or something. It's even worse for Sandy. I finally found a woman that knows me and can give as good as she gets. We've made enough money here to keep us going for a long time. If nothing else, you were right about this place."

Sandy came gracefully down the stairs in her new dress. I

don't know enough about women's fashion to describe what she was wearing, but it sure enough took my breath away. The long dress was a copper color that set off her black hair and blue eyes like nothing else I had ever seen. A high, white lace collar almost made her look like a desert flower. She had a stylish hat and a parasol and I couldn't believe what I saw. Neither could Robert.

"My God," he breathed. "I have never seen a more beautiful woman in all my days. Sandy, my love, you are gorgeous."

She beamed at him. "Why thank you, dear. I wanted to make sure you never noticed another woman."

"No problem there," I said. "You are by far the prettiest female in that get-up that ever came through Lexington."

I could tell she was biting her tongue to keep from coming up with a smart remark. "Don't worry. I won't let anybody else know that I gave you a compliment."

"D.W.," she said, controlling herself admirably, "that's the sweetest thing you've ever said to me."

Robert nearly tripped over himself getting to her side. "Let's go show you off to these peons around here."

She cocked her head and looked him straight in the eye. "I'm not going to waste this on the people around here. Did you tell him yet?"

Robert looked back at me and nodded his head yes.

She strolled over to me. "We're going to be gone before winter sets in. Do you want to buy us out?"

"I couldn't buy you out. My wife would cut my balls off and feed 'em to me for breakfast if I tried to run a cathouse. You can take those beds upstairs and sell 'em for all I care. I can't manage no women. As for Robert's tables, he's only got a couple of games that's worth anythin'. I don't know why we'd be puttin' in a new table if you were plannin' on leavin' in the first place."

"Just call it a going-away present," Robert said. "It's the kind of game that anybody can come in and run. Even you could find somebody to do it."

I pursed my lips. "Won't help any, I'm afraid. Sandy's girls was our biggest attraction. Only thing made us different than the rest of the saloons along here. With the marshals sittin' on us, it might be a good time to leave."

Sandy looked alarmed. "Marshals? What marshals?"

"Oh, it seems like the Oklahombres had a shootout with some deputies and killed three of them. Swain is going to send a deputy down to watch over the saloon. He'll be posted in the front room upstairs."

"That's it, Robert. I'm going upstairs and change. Then, I'm going to pack everything I have and move into Lexington. I won't set foot back in this place again."

"That's a relief," I said. "I was worried I wouldn't survive the next couple of months."

Sandy narrowed her eyes. "The only thing that would get me back here is a chance to put a couple of holes in your walrus hide," she said to me.

"See, Robert," I told him, "pretty on the outside don't make `em pretty on the inside."

"Oooh, you half-witted sack of buffalo dung. If I didn't have a better use for my money, I'd hire someone to fill you full of lead." She pulled up her skirts and stomped upstairs.

"Now, why'd you have to go and do that? First, you compliment her and then you insult her," he groaned. "It'll take me two days to calm her down."

"It's easier that way. I'm not much on sentiment. Just ask my wife or my brother," I said, "if you can find him. You wouldn't recognize the two of us if we was nice to each other. What really got you stampeded off in another direction?"

"It's the craziness around here. When we started this place, all we had to worry about was the rough-and-tumble saloon business. I've been all over the Southwest so a few rowdy cowboys and a bunch of drunks and robbers were easy enough to handle. The river doesn't bother me any. I've seen the Mississippi do a hell of a lot more damage than this little stream ever has. But, a year or so ago, it just started getting crazy.

That's when Eugene Robinson died."

"Robinson? I don't recall him."

"He was that gambler that died from a drug overdose. He got drunk and gave himself too much morphine. You remember. They arrested Fred Ferry and Bill Cooper over it. I knew Robinson from a half-dozen saloons here and in Kansas. I don't know how he got snookered into taking morphine, but I could see myself ending up that way if I wasn't careful."

"Oh, hell, you could get a hankerin' for morphine from gettin' thrown off a horse. Them doctors give you enough painkiller and you'll be wantin' that stuff till the day they lay you in the ground. Doesn't have anything to do with the gamblin' as far as I can see," I told him.

"Yeah, but the marshals are getting on my nerves too. Seems like we're getting visited on a regular basis. You remember that raid they made in the Fox building some time ago. Broke up a craps game and chopped up all that guy's equipment."

"That was in Purcell. That's still in Indian Territory. They're selective about who they raid, anyway. The right citizen has to complain to get their attention. That newspaper editor takes a hard line with gamblers and such but you just have to ignore him. The paper worked real hard to get that Chinaman run out of town."

"See. That's another one of those crazy things. Running an opium den, prostitutes and gambling. That's a bad mix."

"So what? A few citizens got up a vigilante posse to run 'em out of town. The Chinaman was supposed to be runnin' a billiard hall. He let anybody in there. Negroes, prostitutes, addicts. The good citizens are goin' to have to go after them every time. Anything that might affect their dainty womenfolk will get 'em riled up enough to do something. Down here in the river, we're far enough away from their sensibilities that they'll leave us alone," I told him.

"Nope. You haven't convinced me. This business with the Oklahombres is another example. We don't have a thing to do with them other than having played a couple of poker games years ago and now the marshals are sitting on top of us. Too many people doing too many crazy things to suit my taste."

"You got to do what your conscience tells you, I guess. I haven't heard mine for some time, so I'm a little out of touch with that part of me. Besides, this ain't any crazier than what goes on in the rest of the country, except maybe for the bank robbers and outlaws. But you can't let a little thing like that bother you. Kansas used to have just as many killin's and some really bad feuds."

Sandy was back downstairs with her dress tucked away in the box. "Let's go, Robert, before I have an urge to breathe the pungent smell of gunsmoke, just one more time."

"It's been nice knowin' you, too. Now maybe that sharp tongue of yours won't be stabbin' any of my customers."

"Hmmph!" she replied. She twirled around and hit the back door going a mile a minute.

Robert started trotting after her. "If anybody comes in for a poker game, send someone to get me. I don't think that deputy is going to help business at all."

Just before sundown, the deputy strolled in. He looked around the saloon and said, "Where is everybody? I thought this place always had some business."

"Sorry to disappoint you," I told him, "but most of my regulars heard you were comin' and they decided they weren't nearly as thirsty as they thought they'd be. It's a waste of your time to be here. Those Oklahombres are a hundred miles away. They don't remember me or this place. Honest."

"Marshal Swain ain't in a mood to listen to any of your chatter. He told me to shoot first and don't bother asking questions. He mentioned that if a few bar patrons accidentally get in the way, not to worry too much about it. He was quite sure he could get the money for funeral expenses. Is that clear?"

"More than you know, deputy."

"After so long a time the road overseer has put in a culvert and otherwise repaired the mudhole, that has long existed, between the sand bar saloon and the First and Last Chance Saloon, and the traveling public are happy. We would call the overseer's attention to another place nearly as bad, just this side of the sand bar and hope in the near future that it will receive the same treatment given the other."

. . . The Purcell Register, March 9, 1894

Chapter 21

There are three things in this world that give a whole new meaning to the word fickle. The first thing is a woman. They are so changeable that it is a wonder that a man is able to maintain any semblance of sanity. One minute you are the best man in the whole world and the next you're crawling out from under some rock and up to no good. The second thing is the weather in the Twin Territories. Not a single other place in the country has weather as contrary as in the middle of these wide open plains. There are some days where you're sweating in the morning and freezing in the middle of an ice storm in the afternoon. One minute the Canadian River is bone dry and the next the water is six feet deep.

Finally, the most fickle thing of all is that selfsame Canadian River. Besides sudden rises in the river, the course of the river tended to wander all over the river bottom. In most places, the river valley is one to two miles wide. In a very short length of time, the river channel could wander from one side to the other taking with it crops, bridges, roads and anything else that hadn't been there since the last time the river came that way. Quicksand, floods, moving river channels, saloons, murders, robberies and alcohol show just how many ways the Canadian River can be fickle.

W.L. Martin of Winfield, Kansas, described it best. "Imagine a river a half a mile wide with not a drop of water in

179

sight, with its broad, dry, white sandy bottom glistening in the morning sun, and then in less time that it requires to tell, see it full fledged, big river, filled with foaming, roaring, lashing muddy water, from three to ten feet deep and you have the whole scene as I saw it this morning. . . .

"Quite a number of cattle were out browsing among the willow bushes that grow at intervals in the river bed and many of them that were caught napping had to swim for the shore, not a few of which were never able to reach dry land, but were overcome by the massive flood and carried down stream by this rush of water. I often heard of such a scene as this but never saw anything like if before, and I shall always remember my visit to Purcell on September 29, 1891."

I had always kept that nailed to the wall behind the bar, just in case anybody wondered why they had to get a move on when somebody yelled, "Bail out," in the middle of a poker game or a bottle of whiskey.

Every time there is a rise in the river that runs bank to bank, the river channel changes. In just the five years since Sand Bar Town poured its first drink, the river had been moving slowly eastward towards Lexington. That had its good points and its bad points. As the river moved in that direction, it brought the saloons closer to the north bank. The customers didn't have as far to go to safety during a flood. However, it meant that the customers had farther to walk to get to the saloons and to go home. That river bottom gets mighty dark at night and the robbers didn't have to do much to take their money. When there was no moon, the thieves fell all over themselves to get at the drunks.

To attract customers, I had to have a gimmick. Then, one day, it floated onto the riverbed.

Thump. Whump. Clump, clump, clump, clump, clump.

I glanced up at the roof wondering what in the hell was going just as everything in the saloon went dark. I grabbed my shotgun and ran out the back door and looked up at the roof.

My mouth hung open in amazement as I saw a man standing on the edge of the roof with some kind of weird contraption draped over the front of the saloon.

"I say, old chap," he called down. "Could you get a ladder and help me remove my flying machine from the roof of your establishment?"

"Your what?"

"My flying machine. My balloon, if you will. I seem to have lost control somewhat and ventured into a rather compromising position," he said.

"Who in the hell are you?"

"Ahhh. You're right. I have forgotten my manners in the distress from my ungainly landing. My name is Waldo Torrington. Waldo the Great. Perhaps you have heard of me? A master of prestidigitation and a sojourner in the skies. Late of Queen Victoria's court in London where I amused the queen with my talents. I have been traveling this great land of yours putting on exhibitions and providing you colonists with some entertainment."

I reached up and scratched the back of my head. "That sounds mighty purty. But, you make a much bigger mess than just about anybody I ever met."

"Charmed, I'm sure."

I waved at him. "Well, don't rush off. I'll be back in a minute or two."

By the time I came back out, a crowd had gathered and two or three of the good colonists were laughing and pointing. I didn't have a ladder, but I stacked a few barrels and boxes against the side of the saloon to form a kind of stairway. Two or three of the boys that weren't laughing climbed up with me and helped move the balloonist off my roof.

When everyone was back down, I yelled, "Drinks for those who were on the house." I spent the next thirty minutes explaining I didn't offer drinks on the house to the lookers-on who stayed on the ground. The first one to the bar, of course, was Waldo the Great.

"I can't believe that you'd be flyin' around Oklahoma Territory if you were as famous as you say," I told him after most of the crowd had left.

"Ahhh. My good man, for another drink, I'll gladly tell you my saga."

"This ought to be good," I answered. I knew better, but I poured him a drink anyway.

"Even though I was one of the queen's favorites, I was not fully appreciated by others at the court. I had the misfortune of being caught in a tryst with a lady who was betrothed to a member of the royal family. Needless to say, the queen was forced to side against me in this matter."

"Seems to me I heard that Queen Victoria is something of a prude. I don't think she would have put up with somebody havin' an affair with anybody in her court."

"I see you follow events in England. That's true. I was chased out of England at the point of a gun and barely escaped with my life. What money I had when I came here is mostly gone. I've been earning some funds with my skills," he said, smiling.

"What are your skills anyway? What's prestidig. . .? Prestigid. . .? Oh, whatever you said."

"Prestidigitation is the art of sleight of hand. Magic, if you will."

"Card tricks, eh?"

"Not card tricks. I am much, much better than that."

"Well, I tell you what. I'm lookin' for a new partner for the Floatin' Palace Saloon here. And, with your card tricks and balloon, we could give a whole new meanin' to the Floatin' Palace. You could rename your balloon and give rides during the day and then handle the poker tables at night."

"I say, old chap. That doesn't sound like a very profitable undertaking."

"This ain't no funeral parlor. We've got some good customers, but since my two partners headed west, I haven't had anything to bring the customers in. The way this works is that I run the bar and you run the balloon and tables. You keep two-thirds of whatever you make and give me one-third. I get to keep two-thirds of what I make on the bar and give you one-third. That gives you some incentives to work."

"Hmmm. Who was the other party?"

"She ran a cathouse upstairs."

"Oh. I say. This is by far the best offer I have received in my journey across the colonies." He reached across the bar to shake my hand. "You have a new partner. How soon can we start?"

"As soon as you put your balloon away, you can start dealin.'"

"By the way, with whom am I now in partnership? It's not often I do business with a perfect stranger."

"Right, I never did introduce myself. D.W. Sweden. You can call me D.W. I've been in the territories for about ten years. Glad to have you joinin' me."

"No doubt," Waldo answered. "So, you want me to deal under the table, so to speak."

"I wouldn't recommend it. The only speakin' done around here is usually with a six-gun. I once knew a gambler name of Three-Finger Hanson. He got caught cheatin' twice. A Bowie took care of one of his fingers and a bullet through one of his extra aces took care of the other one. After that, he didn't win much but he never earned the moniker of Two-Finger Hanson. If you're a good poker player, you can win. If you don't like that, run the faro table and keep the bank."

"I see. Point made. I shall begin to set the faro table up immediately."

About that time, Skunkbit came in the front door. "You got a balloon outside. Did you know how it got there?"

"Skunkbit, you are as observant as ever. My new partner dropped in. Kind of heaven sent, so to speak. What brings you in so early?"

"Did you hear about Bill Carr?"

"Haven't heard a thing," I replied.

"He's been running a store over at Violet Springs. He got into a shootout the other day. Caught a couple of bullets from what I hear. He's hurt pretty bad."

"Too bad. What happened?"

"These two guys come in his store and he recognized them as a couple of outlaws. He tried to draw down on them, but they shot him. Got him in the right arm. Carr picked up the gun with his left hand and shot one of the bandits. Then he caught a bullet in the gut. That's the one that's got him laid up."

"Did they catch them?"

"Not likely. It was Bill Dalton and Slaughter's Kid. These marshals aren't any closer to catching them than they were last year after that shootout in Ingalls."

"Slaughter's Kid. That sounds familiar. Oh, yeah, that's what they called Bitter Creek Newcomb. I'm goin' to have to take his name off'n my bar if he keeps shootin' old friends."

"I don't want to be around those boys again," Skunkbit said. "They're bad medicine anymore."

"You got that right. We have enough trouble without addin' them."

Waldo walked, well, more like strolled back into the saloon. "This here is Waldo the Great. He runs the gamblin' tables and gives out balloon rides. Waldo, this here is Skunkbit. He's lived around here since before there was even a Purcell. Right?"

"You bet," Skunkbit nodded and held out his hand.

Waldo sniffed and then extended his hand. "Charmed, I'm sure."

Skunkbit shook the hand and then headed towards the door. "See you later. I've got a few more stops to make."

"One of your better customers?" Waldo asked.

"Nah. He don't drink much and don't gamble. But I've known him a long time and he gets more gossip than the widow women up on Second Street in Purcell."

"How come you landed on my roof? I thought you balloon-ists always kept a tether rope on your balloons."

"I take it I'm not the first one to come through with such a flying exhibition."

"Not at all. The saloon owners in Purcell brought in a bal-loonist a few years ago trying to take a little business away from Sand Bar Town. It didn't work too well, though. The weather put a dent in their plans rather quickly. I don't think that guy came down until he reached Louisiana," I said laughing.

"That's not that funny."

I still couldn't help laughing. "That fellow didn't listen when they told him about those storm fronts. The guys that were holdin' the rope were pulled off the ground by a gust of wind. A couple of them held on until the rope dragged them through the first tree. Then a dozen or so cowboys got on their horses and started chasin' the balloon tryin' to shoot it down. You could hear that balloonist screaming in terror until he was out of sight. They finally brought him down when the wind tore a hole in the balloon. I've never seen anybody as white as that guy was when they brought him back. I understand he never went up in a balloon again."

"Charming."

"Hey, you know, that balloon of yours could come in handy. You could get up in it and see floods comin' a lot further away."

"Floods?"

"Sure. After all, we are in a riverbed. But don't worry. We've got one of the biggest boats on the river."

"That's why this saloon is so odd," he said.

"Now, why did you land on my roof?"

"It seems I met yet another disgruntled lover of a female who swooned over me. Little did I know that her lover would cut my guy line."

"You should watch your step around these parts. They'd just as soon shoot you as look at you. And, chasin' a skirt is one easy way to get into trouble. It's just not healthy to take chances like that."

"So, I've noticed. However, this time was not of my doing. I did not encourage the young woman in the least. I only realized the danger when I looked down the line and saw her trying to grab the man's arm. He threw her away and sliced the line. It was a new way of casting one's fate to the wind."

After his first night at the faro table, Waldo was relatively happy. I convinced him to spend the night upstairs rather than try to go back to Lexington. A couple of gunshots and a scream seemed to help him make up his mind. The following day was the first opportunity for the new partnership to take off, so to speak.

Waldo showed up shortly after the noon hour the next day, looking relatively well rested. "I say, old chap," he said. "That's more money in one night than I have seen for many days. How large a percentage do I have to pay you for the balloon business?"

"Nothin.' Whatever you make on that contraption is yours to keep. I'll make my money from the booze I'll sell when they come to watch. Just don't crash it too many times. That would be bad for business."

"I'll have you know that landing on your roof was the first accident I ever had. My flying skills are second to none. Don't worry. We'll be ready to go. Did you want to make the first flight?"

"Not on your life. I have enough trouble walkin.' I ain't about to start on learnin' how to fly."

"It's your loss. I shall need a place to anchor my tether."

"There's a post out the back door you can tie off to."

"Excellent."

He went out and I could hear him puttering around. An hour or so later I heard a thump against the back wall and went out to see what was going on. I walked out and saw the line pulled tight against the wall. I looked up and could see the balloon a long ways up in the air. I shook my head, wondering what kind of a fool it was that left solid ground for a basket under a balloon. I couldn't see Waldo, but I figured he was doing okay. I heard some voices and looked towards Lexington. Sure enough, folks were starting to come down to the saloon. I got busy and rolled out a couple of barrels on the front porch and put a couple of boards across them and set up an outdoors bar. For the first time in a long time, the Floating Palace Saloon had a lot of customers in the afternoon.

Waldo winched the balloon down about halfway and leaned over the side. "Who wants a bird's-eye view of the Canadian River valley. Step up to the bar and lay down one dollar and ride to the heavens with the Floating Palace balloon."

A couple of young bucks came up and plunked down their money. I could tell they were doing this on a dare. I leaned out and yelled up, "You got a couple of customers." He leaned out and smiled. Waldo winched back down and climbed out.

"Who's going first?" he asked. The youngest looking cowboy stepped up. "You must leave your weapon on the ground."

"I never go anywhere without my pistol," he said, bowing his back.

"I am sorry. However, I have found that people often get overly excited on their first ascent. I have no desire to have you pull out your weapon and fire into the air to express your elation. Shooting holes in the balloon produces a detrimental effect on its ability to stay aloft."

"Huh," the cowboy responded.

"It means if you shoot a hole in the balloon, you'll crash," his friend said.

"All right. I'll leave my gun, but Ben here has to hold it," the cowboy said.

"Fine. Step right in," Waldo said. The cowboy looked at the basket and then his friend who was sitting there with a grin on his face. He swallowed and stepped into the basket. Waldo started paying the line out and I could see the cowboy had a death grip on the sides of the basket and his eyes were closed. A few minutes later, the balloon halted its rise. A couple of minutes later, the cowboy let out a whoop that could be heard in Norman. He got so excited the basket started jumping back and forth. After Waldo got the guy calmed down, they stayed up a few more minutes before he winched it back down.

As soon as he touched ground, he started talking, "You can't believe how it feels up in the sky. It's smoother than a paddle-wheel boat ride. I could see all the way to Wayne down south and Noble up north. Those people in Purcell looked like ants scurrying around. I've never done anything like that before in my life. That's the greatest feeling I've ever had."

His friend handed the cowboy his gunbelt and then unbuck-led his own. He climbed in the balloon without any hesitation. "Let's go," he told Waldo.

After that, the number of clients for balloon rides rose dra-matically. Along with all those balloon rides came all those drinks. We finally had to put in a rule that if you couldn't walk straight you couldn't take a balloon ride. Waldo almost lost a couple of them over the side. One of the drunks threw up from the basket and that was all it took. Besides, they were a lot thirstier when they came down.

Balloon. Saloon. The Floating Palace was back in business.

"The repairs at the Canadian bridge are still under way, with a large force of hands engaged. The south bank is being very greatly strengthened by putting in rip rap, several hundred cars of stone having already been used for this purpose and work not nearly half completed."

The Purcell Register, Jan. 26, 1894

Chapter 22

If you ever get comfortable with what you are up to in life and you're just beginning to enjoy it, you are in a perfect position to get run over by progress. All the old sailing ships were replaced by steamships. The Indians were done in by railroad locomotives. And, Sand Bar Town was done in by a bridge. It wasn't a very big bridge mind you, but it was enough to get folks out of the riverbed and straight into Lexington safe, sound and dry.

As bridges go, this one was downright ugly. The people who built the bridge had to build piers every forty or fifty feet because the sands were so treacherous. Then they just laid a plank floor across the bridge beams. A railing was put up and the bridge was open for business. It wasn't a very tall bridge, but it would do until something better came along. The only good thing was that the bridge was only big enough to let one wagon across at a time. That means you had to send somebody across the river to stop oncoming wagons or carriages. There were some really good fights at the ends of the bridges. They finally had to put toll booths at either end of the bridge. They set up a flag system to let either end of the bridge know who was waiting.

A lot of the freight haulers still came across the riverbottom because it was closer to the railroad depot. But the bars in Lexington now could set up hack service from Purcell without having to go through Sand Bar Town. That was what really began to hurt our traffic to Sand Bar Town. By the end of summer, the Canadian River had already dried up and the libation

189

business wasn't far behind.

Waldo came in from outside, sweat dripping off his face. He took out a handkerchief and wiped his brow. "I say, old chap, this summer weather of yours tends to stay hot for an awfully long time. I didn't realize how much this heat slows down everything. When will the weather break?"

"No problem," I told him. "We're just about to head into tornado season. That'll cool things off in ways you can't even imagine. When those storms come roarin' through, you'll feel like you've been run over by a freight train. That rain is so cold you'd think it was almost wintertime. And hail. The hailstones are so big they can brain a bull buffalo. Yeah, you're goin' to love the change in weather."

"I must say that doesn't do much for my sense of prosperity. The novelty has worn off the balloon rides, I'm afraid. It's almost not worth the trouble it takes to show up every day during the week. The weekends are the only time I can make any money," he lamented.

"Well, I guess you could take your balloon up Depot Hill and give the ladies a ride. You don't have to stay down here all the time."

"You don't sound very optimistic either."

"Let's lock up and go for a walk," I said.

We headed for the east end of the new bridge. The trees were a pale shade of green. The leaves were all curled up in the oppressive heat. There was a thick layer of dust on everything and the riverbed sand was powder fine and hard to walk through. Looking up the river, you could see mirages rising in the heat waves off the sand. Those big wide-brimmed cowboy hats were the only thing that gave any shade at all. I plopped down the toll and started walking out on the bridge.

The cloudless sky was a pale blue as though the sun had bleached the color out of it too. There wasn't anything stirring anywhere along the river and not much in the town.

"We're standin' on the reason business is goin' downhill," I told Waldo. When we got to the middle of the bridge, we stopped. I leaned on the rail and looked downriver to Sand Bar Town. The clapboard on the buildings had turned an ashy gray. "Don't look like much anymore, if it ever did. Progress is passin' it by."

"So what are you going to do about that."

"I'm goin' back to the farm and make sure my kids don't run out of things to do. There's a few things we can do. The saloon business won't last much longer."

"How can you tell?"

"Civilization has set down in the territories. Prohibition is on its way. They've got preachers and politicians workin' on gettin' rid of the liquor business."

"I say, that would take all the fun out of this type of enterprise. I dare say that you're wrong."

"No. I've watched this happen in other towns where the folks just flat got tired of all the shenanigans that go with the drinkin'. There's too many outlaws and too many shootin's and these folks have to blame something. What with the sad state of Indian affairs, it'll come about."

"This doesn't seem to be such an impressive structure. Nothing at all like the Tower Bridge in London. I think you overestimate it's impact," Waldo said. "This will be here years from now."

"Maybe."

We walked on over into Purcell. Waldo went off to find a new site for his balloon rides. I hadn't been up on Red Hill in a long time, so I wandered off up the road and found my favorite tree. The late afternoon sun warmed me as I sat under the tree. I was off daydreaming about something when a wisp of a cool breeze got my attention. I looked to the northwest and saw a line of dark clouds hugging the horizon. In the few minutes, I watched, the clouds began to boil up and climb up the western sky. The wind kicked up some puffs of dust. I knew it was time to go back to the saloon and get ready for a new storm.

I was in the back room hanging up my hat when the front door opened and closed. I yelled, "Be with you in a minute." I could hear glasses clinking on the bar and I got a little upset. Then, I thought it must be Waldo. When I walked out, I saw two people outlined in the front window.

"Hey, what's goin' on."

"I told you we shouldn't have come here, Robert. Take your gun out and shoot him," I heard a less than melodious voice say.

"Well, look what the cat dragged in. Hello, Sandy. Robert, how the hell are you? I wasn't expectin' to ever see you again," I said, grabbing Robert's hand and pumping it up and down.

"We're on our way to New Orleans," Robert said. "We've bought a gambling house down there. We're going to make our home there."

"Amazin.' How come you stopped here? Sandy get thrown off the train for her bad mouth," I said laughing.

"It wasn't my idea. I have a hard enough time keeping my breakfast down just being in the same general area as you, let alone the same room."

"I'm glad to see you haven't changed any. The place hasn't been the same without you."

"Who's the guy out back?" Robert asked.

"That's my new partner, Waldo the Great."

"The only thing great around here is the size of the mosquitoes," Sandy chimed in. "What makes him great?"

"He's a balloonist. Added a whole new dimension to the Floating Palace. You can have a ride if you want."

Sandy's eyes started to shine. Robert took one look at her and said, "Not again. I'm not going with you this time."

"Oh, please. You haven't done anything exciting since we went skiing in the Rocky Mountains."

"We almost got killed," he said plaintively. "The people around there hadn't seen an avalanche like that for over forty years."

"It was wonderful."

I smiled. I was glad to see that Robert still didn't have any control over her. "I'll go get Waldo. He's gettin' ready to move it up to Purcell, but I'm sure he can do a quick ride now, if you want."

"Oh, I do," Sandy cooed.

I walked out back with Sandy on my heels and Robert slowly bringing up the rear. "Hey, Waldo. How long would it take to get your balloon up for a ride?"

"Not long. I have it half filled so I can float it up the hill. Is this the person who wants the ride?"

Sandy came out the back door and she had eyes only for that balloon. It was wavering a bit in the wind. The sky was just beginning to get dark above Red Hill. "This here is Sandy and Robert. They're my former partners. Sandy has a thing for excitement, it seems."

"My dear lady, you've come to the right place."

"I'd hurry it up, Waldo. That cool weather I was talkin' about is comin' in from the northwest at a pretty fast clip. This will have to be a quick trip."

"No problem," he said. "I'll have the balloon ready to go in five minutes."

"How did you guys do in Denver?" I asked Robert.

"We were doing well until a fire wiped out half the district. We lost all our equipment and most of our clothes. We still have some money, but those winters were a bit too much for us. I got a telegram from an old gambling friend who was tired of being tied down to one place and was looking for a buyer. He knew I was up here and wanted me to come look. It came at a good time. We were headed for Kansas City. But when we got to Wichita and I said let's go to Dallas. That'll take us through Purcell. Believe it or not, this riverbed is still the best place I've ever worked."

"It ain't what it used to be," I told him. "They finally put a bridge in and a lot of traffic goes that way now. Brought in the balloon and that boosted business for awhile. But, that's no big deal anymore. He's movin' it up to Purcell to see if he can get some of the ladies to pay for some rides. Gamblin' and liquor just don't get 'em down off that bridge anymore. Those hacks take 'em straight into Lexington high and dry."

"It's ready," Sandy shrieked, jumping up and down in anticipation. "This is going to be fun."

We watched as she climbed into the balloon and Waldo started paying out the line. Once the balloon got up above the riverbed, the wind started to catch it. We could hear Sandy's laughter. She was fine until she looked off to the northwest. I could see her pointing and I knew she was saying something to Waldo. There was a shriek, this time, and the balloon started coming down rapidly.

I looked at Robert. "The only thing that makes her scream like that is a flood."

We looked at each other and then upriver. The bridge was a thin brown line drawn across a black wall. "Oh, hell," Robert responded. "Let's get them down."

By this time, Sandy was low enough that we could hear her. "Come on. Get this balloon down." She leaned over the basket, "Robert, you wouldn't believe the flood that's coming. I haven't ever seen anything like it. Let's go. We've got to get out of here."

"The storm isn't even close," I said. "There shouldn't be a flood comin.'"

"Well there is," she screamed. "I still can't swim and I'm damned if I'm going to die in this damned river."

A low roar began to grow in strength. Waldo had the balloon down to roof level when we heard a horrible groan and crash. A quick glance showed the bridge was gone. I grabbed Robert and headed inside. "Stay in the balloon. We're going upstairs. Moments later, the wall of water struck Sand Bar Town. The Floating Palace shuddered once and then started shaking. Robert and I got to the front room and opened a window to climb out on the porch roof. The water had boiled down the river so quickly that it sloshed over the sides of the barge before it had even had a chance to start floating. Robert and I clambered up on the roof. Sandy was beating Waldo, while trying to get out of the balloon basket.

"Stay there," Robert yelled. "We're coming."

We ran across the roof and reached the balloon basket. Robert grabbed a rope and threw his leg over the edge of the basket. He was halfway in the basket and turned back to me. "Come on. What are you waiting for?"

"I ain't sure this is such a good idea," I said, hesitating a few feet from the basket. A section of the bridge came barreling down the river on the flood crest, crashing into the side of the saloon and collapsing the right front corner. The balloon lurched and swayed closer to me. Robert grabbed one arm and Waldo grabbed the other and heaved me into the basket. I went in head first and my legs were sticking up in the air, waving like crazy.

"Cut the line," Waldo yelled at Sandy. Suddenly the balloon shot upwards. Waldo jumped to the control lines to try to control the ascent.

"Would you look at that," Sandy breathed. "That is incredible."

Robert finally got me turned right side up and I edged up the side of the basket. I didn't know how high up we were but it must have been a mile high. I blinked my eyes and damn near fainted. The balloon was rising smoothly. I could see Purcell and Lexington behind us. I didn't understand exactly what I was seeing.

"Unbelievable," Robert said. "Water is up in the depot already. Main Street in Lexington is under water too. Damn, there goes the Floating Palace."

"Where," I croaked.

He pointed down the side of the balloon. All I could see was the roof riding the flood tide down river. I blinked my eyes. A mile or so downriver, the riverbed was still dry. The front edge of the flood was a churning roil of dirty brown water and white foam. I turned my head and watched as each section of the bridge popped up out of the water as the flood broke them free from the piers. At that point, I groaned and sank down to the bottom of the basket.

"Poor man," Sandy said. "Now he knows how I feel when a flood is coming."

"Boy, Waldo, this is beautiful," Robert said.

"Quite, old chap, although I don't recommend this as the best way to become a balloonist. I couldn't get D.W. up in the balloon until this moment. I don't believe that he will be interested in another ride."

"That storm is moving in spurts and fits. I think that's why the river was able to outrun the storm," Robert said. "But we need to get down before it makes its final run."

"Right you are," Waldo replied. "I need to release the gas for a slow descent. Unfortunately, the guiding winds are keeping us over the river. I don't want to get too low until I am sure we are over land.

A huge gust of wind swept us east of the river and Waldo completed the descent. We landed in a grove of persimmon trees. The basket hit the ground and everyone jumped out but me. The balloon pulled the basket over and I rolled out on the ground. I kneeled on the ground and kept saying over and over again, "Solid ground. Solid ground."

A few big cold drops of rain finally shocked me out of my state. Waldo and Robert had taken the balloon and made a tent out of it. They were sitting inside just watching me. I scrambled over to the makeshift tent just as the storm broke overhead. Rain pounded down on the balloon and the wind howled. Once the front passed, the heavens opened up and rain came pouring down. I started laughing.

"There's goin' to be a lot of folks wonderin' what happened to Sand Bar Town. I think I would rather drown than fall out of the sky. I'll take my chances in the water next time. Well,

Waldo, what do you think of all this."

"I never considered myself much of a hero before. I usually ended up running away before I could be confronted by danger. I think its time to go back home."

"To England?"

"To London, yes. Thank you for stopping me in my head-long flight."

"Hmmm. I guess I should thank you for pulling me off that roof. I knew that old river was fickle but I never thought it could do that. There won't be anything at all left of that saloon. I think I'll head for the hills. That's as high as I ever want to get again."

Sandy looked at me. "Well, Robert, I guess you don't have to shoot him. But, I'll tell you again. Putting a saloon in the middle of a river is the craziest idea any lamebrain ever came up with."

Printed in the United States
by Baker & Taylor Publisher Services